# REDMAN RANGE

When he rode towards New Mexico territory, Rusty Redman expected to find the Redmans of Redman City friendly to a man with the same surname. His outlook changed, however, when he found Laura Burke fleeing from her Redman kin, fearing for her life, and witnessed Redman hirelings bullying farmers. In Big Bend, he took up arms against their gunslingers and played a highly dangerous part in bringing law and order back to the ordinary people.

DAVID BINGLEY

# REDMAN RANGE

*Complete and Unabridged*

**LINFORD**
*Leicester*

First published in Great Britain in 1975

First Linford Edition
published 2006

British Library CIP Data

Bingley, David
    Redman Range.—Large print ed.—
Linford western library
1. Western stories
2. Large type books
I. Title II. Horsley, David
823.9′14 [F]

ISBN 1–84617–471–6

Published by
F. A. Thorpe (Publishing)
Anstey, Leicestershire

Set by Words & Graphics Ltd.
Anstey, Leicestershire
Printed and bound in Great Britain by
T. J. International Ltd., Padstow, Cornwall

This book is printed on acid-free paper

# 1

The card-playing gamblers were in a private room at the back of a large saloon known as the Wagoners' Rest in a town called Prairie City, in the Texas Panhandle. The gaming had started early in the afternoon when the townsfolk who only used the building for drinking and gossip had started to thin out.

After two hours, four bottles of whisky had been emptied, and countless cigarettes and cigars had combined to fill the upper atmosphere with a blue haze of smoke. There were two tables. The four nondescript trail riders at the far one against the wall which sported the moose's head had kept themselves to themselves, showing no particular interest in the goings on at the other.

And yet Rusty Redman was sure that they were familiar with two of the men at his table of four.

Prairie City was a free and easy place in regard to the carrying of firearms and, as was customary, regular gamblers had to carry an armoury. Rusty had only met his fellow players that same morning, but already he felt he knew quite a lot about them. Richy Malone and Skinner Grouch were gambling partners. Richy was a tall, big-boned fellow dressed in a battered top hat and a dark shiny frockcoat over a red double-breasted waistcoat. He had small dark, restless eyes, and a down-drooping walrus moustache which camouflaged his big jaw. He had a revolver at his waist and a smaller weapon, probably a Derringer, in a holster under his left arm. He handled the cards easily with long spatulate fingers and showed no emotions about the game's fluctuations.

Skinner Grouch sat opposite him, a small fat swarthy character with a long crescent of close-cropped moustache balanced across his thick upper lip. He chain-smoked short cigars and seemed impervious to the heat in the room. His coonskin hat was still on his head. The handle of a broad-bladed knife, sheathed in a belt worn diagonally across his barrel chest, moved this way and that as his short arms went through the motions of picking up and discarding the pasteboards.

The fourth player answered to the name of Willie Small. He had recently paid off as a waddie on a ranch some distance away. He claimed that Prairie City was his home town. At the commencement of the game he had removed his dun stetson and placed a green eyeshade above his eyes. Whether his eyes suffered in the glare of the overhanging lamp, or he wanted to look like a professional was not clear.

'I guess that's your game, Skinner,' Richy commented, in a deep throaty voice. 'Seems your luck's changed for the better.'

Skinner rolled his cigar butt round to the corner of his mouth with his

3

tongue, coughed a few times and started to gather the coin and paper money stacked in the centre of the table towards himself.

The chairs creaked as the players shifted their positions.

Rusty beat a silent tattoo with his fingers on the table. He had lost three successive games and the money he had put aside for gambling, plus his winnings from earlier games, had now gone to others. Richy had a prosperous heap in front of him. Skinner's pile was growing. Small whipped off his hat and mussed up his thinning red hair. He was down to some twenty-odd dollars and his perspiring face showed the tension which gripped him.

'You want to deal, Rusty?' Skinner enquired.

Rusty made up his mind quickly. He wondered how they would take his decision. 'Nope. As of now, folks, count me out. I've lost all I can afford. Gambling is only an occasional occupation. I don't have the professional's skill. Or his luck.'

He thought he detected a slight extra tension in the air as he pronounced the word 'luck'. At the next table, two chairs moved a fraction as though the players were making preparations for something or another.

A few more seconds went by slowly. Rusty reached for the back of his chair and prepared to stand up.

Malone lifted his top hat and yawned inelegantly into it.

'Shucks, that's too bad, Rusty. I was gettin' used to playin' alongside of you. Sure you won't have a shot of whisky, if we can't persuade you to play on?'

On his feet, Rusty suddenly grinned and gestured with his hand in a negative fashion. 'No. No whisky, thanks. No I don't need a cigar, Skinner. I know I've lost but I don't feel too badly about it. Guess I'll take a stroll in what passes for fresh air around these parts. *Adios*, and thanks.'

The three remaining players chorused their farewells, while two men at the other table, seemingly more intent upon his withdrawal than the state of their game, nodded to him. Rusty negotiated the one door of the room, stepping into the main part of the saloon and surveying the tables, which were mostly empty.

A tired pale-faced barman was mechanically wiping down the far end of the long counter. At the near end, two men were asleep on stools with their heads lolling forward on to the bar top. Two or three tables were still occupied by men who studied their beer rather than pouring it thirstily down their necks. Rusty walked casually along the front of the bar. His image in the long mirror behind it kept him company.

He was a tall, lean upstanding young man in his middle twenties. The nickname of Rusty had nothing at all to do with hair colouring. In fact, it was an abbreviation for his Christian name, Russell. His hair was dark enough to be almost bluish, trimmed fairly short and parted at the left side. His face was clean-shaven, except where his square-cut sideburns extended down his cheeks. His nose was slightly Roman in profile over a lean firm mouth.

Although he could claim to be a man of the trails, his black wide-brimmed flat-crowned stetson was well brushed. The dark blue cloth vest which topped a shirt of a paler colour looked neat on him, as did the white bandanna at his neck.

'Two beers, barman.'

The automatic bar cleaning went on for a few seconds, until a certain sharpness in the customer's eye-glance prompted a response. Rusty paid for the drinks, moved to a table near the batwings and there sat himself down and removed his hat. In the mildest of breezes, he started to sip the lukewarm beer.

His thoughts were still in the gaming room. During the last two games he had felt sure he was being cheated. Malone and Grouch had worked well.

If they had had any sort of communication system going for them, he had not detected it. Nor had he found anything wrong with the yellowing pasteboards used for the games. About a half hour earlier, he had thought about protesting, but discretion had made him think again. If, as he thought, the other four players at the further table were in league with Malone and Grouch, a tricky situation could have developed.

Any suggestion of cheating usually provoked fighting, and professional gamblers did not carry their weapons for show. It would have been six-to-one against if it had come to a showdown. Small, very likely, would have remained neutral.

Rusty would have liked to know their system, but that was asking too much. He wondered if discretion was cowardly, in the face of such odds. Shrugging, he reapplied himself to the beer. It did nothing to slake his thirst and only made him more drowsy.

His mind slipped away from the card

players and his thoughts settled on himself, his travels and speculation about the future.

He had been reared in Wichita, Kansas. His folks were second generation Americans. Some six months earlier, pleading letters from England where the Redmans' ancestors had lived for a couple of centuries, had finally drawn his mother and father back to the old country.

He had elected to stay in the United States. With his folks gone from Wichita, he had become restless. He had tired of working for local ranchers and following a chance conversation with a travelling salesman concerning a town called Redman City, west of the Pecos, he had pulled up his young roots and taken to the trails, determined to investigate for himself this other clan of Redman stock who had given the name to a thriving township.

He smiled unconsciously, as he thought of the possible welcome he might receive from a whole lot of thriving Redmans with a soft spot for a distant 'cousin' who could handle cows and horses and do a variety of cowtown jobs. He was still smiling when the beer was finished. He stood up, ran his thumbs around the inside of his trousers at belt level and casually shouldered his way through the batwings into the street.

The sun was high and brassy. There was little movement of humans or of animals. In the shade afforded by the sidewalk awnings on his side of the street men were taking their *siestas* on the benches and propped against the wall. He glanced about him, envied them, although he had never been a man for sleeping in the afternoon. He had been brought up to think that *siestas* were a Mexican habit, and not the sort of laziness a well brought-up white American ought to indulge in.

He started down the street, stepping carefully. There was a thump behind him. An elderly man with a face like seamed leather had rolled off his bench

10

to a rude awakening on the boards. The fellow was about to climb back again, but his bladder bade him to do otherwise. He retreated up the street at a slow pace. The way his boots scuffed under the outsize poncho suggested that he would not have the energy to make it back again.

Rusty thought about following him. He glanced back at the empty bench, and the desire to rest overcame other considerations. He backtracked and stretched his long body out on the crude resting place, tilting his hat over his eyes. It was just wide enough to take his shoulder-blades.

In five minutes, he was asleep.

★   ★   ★

Nothing happened for a long time to disturb him, and when noise and movement returned to the sidewalk and the saloon, he was slow to regain consciousness. He was aware of comings and goings, and some time later men on the move with greater urgency and with their voices raised. Lethargy and the beer made him impervious to excitement for a while longer.

It was not until a hand removed his .45 Colt from the holster at his right hip that he began to have the impression that he was in some way involved. Without opening his eyes, he began slowly to marshal his thoughts. He had a fleeting impression that someone had touched him in passing some time earlier. And then this. Unless he was dreaming his gun had been lifted, and that, according to any standards, was serious.

Harsh tobacco breath near his face made him wrinkle his nostrils. A clumsy hand lifted his hat and stuck it back in place again.

A voice said: 'Kyle, I'm certain sure this was one of the gamblers in the back room!'

The tobacco breath was withdrawn and someone else, breathing through his mouth, came closer. The tip of a bandanna brushed Rusty's chin. Suddenly, he felt incensed. He reached up, grabbed the cloth, stuck his knee in the stomach of the man hauled towards him and, with a sudden muscular effort, caused the other to somersault over his head. During the effort, Rusty lost his own hat and released his grip. His victim landed heavily on the boards, bouncing on his backside and cracking his bared head against the front wall of the saloon.

Rusty sprang to his feet, his right hand going down to his empty holster. He glared at the elderly man with the broken brown teeth and tobacco breath. About six others, armed and businesslike were backing him up.

'What in tarnation is goin' on in this place? Prairie City is no use to a visitor if he can't take a short *siesta* unmolested, an' that's for sure!'

A cascade of thin light objects fell from Rusty's waistband, scattering on the boards. Rusty was even more startled than the others. His straight brows climbed his forehead as he recognized the cards he had been playing with in the back room.

Deputy Kyle Waters' homely features were so contorted by rage that his mouth kept opening and shutting as he replaced his stetson and the badge dislodged from his shirt. He pushed his gun back into its holster and recovered Rusty's weapon which had slipped out of his waist belt.

'Such a visitor is certain sure headed for trouble if he lays hands on a peace officer the way you jest did, hombre!'

He scrambled to his feet with his hat at a strange angle on his shock of springy brown hair. The cream head-gear had suffered in the encounter. Even the deputy's stiff handlebar moustache had collected a lot of dust.

Rusty wrenched his thoughts away from the playing cards and faced up to him. 'Where I come from a man is excused almost anything if he is brutally attacked in his sleep! What's the idea grabbin' my gun while I'm sleepin'? Has the law gone feeble in these parts?'

Rusty's sarcasm was wasted.

'You've jest shed a deck of cards, an' we're lookin' for a murderin' bunch of card gamblers right at this instant!'

'They're not *my* cards,' Rusty retorted. The deputy's words had caused him to feel very uneasy. 'I reckon they were planted on me while I slept! *You* could have done it, if you were anxious for an arrest!'

Deputy Waters faced him, eye to eye. 'It jest so happens I didn't plant them on you, stranger.'

'Then somebody else did!' the accused fumed. His gaze fell upon the elderly tobacco chewer, who backed away a yard or more. At the same time, three other men lined their revolvers upon Rusty and made it clear they were ready to use them.

Waters said, 'Take him up to the office, boys. The marshal an' some of the others will soon find where his buddies are skulkin'. Small's death won't go unavenged for very long.'

Rusty placed his hands on his hips. Clearly, he recognized that this was not the time for further protest. He glanced around the ring of guns.

'Are you sayin' that Willie Small is dead?'

The tobacco chewer was the one who condescended to nod. From a safe distance he was getting a big kick out of his silent reply. He had seen a lot of hangings in his time. Already he was seeing a rope around the stranger's neck, in place of the white bandanna.

# 2

Only five minutes were needed for Rusty to be marched to the town marshal's office and lodged in the 'immediately available' cell fronting into the office itself. For a time, he stood behind the bars fuming and berating the deputy, but his harsh words and his protests got him nowhere.

Suddenly he dried up, and the attendant guns who had escorted him along to the office began to lose interest.

Deputy Waters threw himself into the marshal's chair with a loud sigh, like a man who has done a heavy day's work. He was ambitious and looking for opportunities and, clearly, he had a few willing supporters in the town who thought he would make a good marshal when the senior man retired.

He busied himself with the cards which had fallen from the prisoner's waist belt. Obviously, he knew more about cheating at cards than Rusty did. He turned to the three men who had acted as temporary deputies.

'See those, boys? When you line them all up together the key cards have a different top edge.'

There was a murmur of interest from the trio near the street door. The old tobacco chewer, who answered to Methuselah, stayed by the window, more intent upon the doings in the street rather than the deputy's discoveries.

Waters held up a card to a ray of sunlight. No sign of holes in the pasteboard at all, but when he studied the pattern on the back he found small but ingenious differences in the make-up of flowers and the number of their leaves. He intimated as much to his cronies, knowing that the prisoner was hearing everything.

'Playin' with a pack like this, the

owner could hardly lose,' he added pointedly.

The eyes of the others turned towards the figure crouched in a seated position behind the bars. They knew Rusty had been checked for secret weapons, but the contents of his pockets had not been turned out.

Without raising his head, Rusty murmured: 'If you're wonderin' about me, I lost. That was why I finished playin' over an hour ago, before all this trouble started.'

There was a noise of men shouting, out in the street. Old Methuselah started to chuckle to himself. The effort he made started him coughing, so that when Waters enquired if there was any sign of the marshal returning he had to reply in sign language. Eventually, the old lookout managed to get control of himself. By that time, four or five animated faces were pressed against the window.

'Ain't no sign of the marshal, no sign at all, Kyle, but there's a whole lot of other fellows linin' up outside. I think I can guess what they have in mind. At least two of them have brought a lariat. Ain't that thoughtful of them, now?'

Talk of the rope made Rusty untie the white square draped round his neck and mop his forehead and face with it. He found himself perspiring unduly and hoping that the town marshal was a much more reasonable man than his deputy. His mind was as full of speculation as that of anyone else in the building. Would the marshal succeed in arresting Malone and Grouch, or would he come back without them and attempt to heap all the guilt on to him — Rusty Redman?

Heavy hands started to thump on the wall beyond the window. Deputy Waters came slowly to his feet. He glanced at the rack of shoulder weapons screwed to a wall. His cronies expected him to do something if the crowd got out of hand, but he knew how difficult it was to control a bunch of men intent upon a blood-letting.

Instead of going out to talk to them, he turned his back upon them, fished out a tobacco sack and began to roll for himself a thick cigarette. Rusty perceived his indecision. It did nothing to take away the prisoner's apprehensiveness.

Rusty fervently hoped that the marshal would get back real soon, with or without the real perpetrators of the crime.

* * *

Ten minutes later, Marshal Jed Trusk pushed his way through the crowd in front of his office. He was fifty years of age, grey-haired, tired and breathing hard, following his mounted exertions in an effort to pick up the trail of the other gamblers. He had failed after making two circuits of the town and he was in a bad humour.

He was blowing hard under his greying black moustache as he created a passage for himself with the barrel of his rifle.

'Why don't you folks stop crowdin' my office door? Can't you see I'm more than passin' busy? Get about your business! I'll let you know when there's any news about significant arrests!'

Somebody called out that Kyle Waters had done his job for him, but he ignored the taunt and kept on going until he was through the door and leaning with his back against it.

Waters had tactfully vacated his chair when Methuselah announced Trusk's arrival. 'You didn't happen to locate the other members of the gamblin' gang, marshal?' the deputy enquired.

'No, I didn't. I know they didn't leave town by any of the regular routes, an' I'm almost certain they ain't holed up anywhere inside the town boundaries. We all know what that means, don't we?'

Waters adjusted the marshal's chair, as the senior man plodded towards it. 'They left by Rustlers' Gully, marshal.

Are you plannin' to follow them that way?'

Trusk flopped into his chair. He studied Rusty for a few seconds and then turned his attention back to the deputy.

'You're young and ambitious, Kyle. Ain't you goin' to volunteer to lead the pursuit up the gully?'

Waters was slow to answer. Trusk, meanwhile, turned his attention to the prisoner. Waters then replied by outlining the flimsy indictment against him. He pointed to the pack of cards on the desk and the two weapons alongside of them. Outside, the shouting and clamouring had died down. A goodly number of men were still hanging about, but they knew Marshal Trusk could not be harassed into making a hasty decision.

In the fleetingly calm period, Rusty spoke up. 'I'm Rusty Redman, travellin' from Wichita, Kansas, to Redman City, New Mexico to link up with folks of the same name as myself,

23

who may or may not be my kin.

'The names of the two gamblers you are lookin' for are Richy Malone an' Skinner Grouch. I never saw them before this mornin' when we met in the coffee house down the street.'

He went on to describe the men in question, and filled in the details from when the gaming had been going on, up until the time of his arrest.

In conclusion, he asked: 'How was Willie Small killed?'

'He was stabbed in the back with a broad-bladed knife. Did either of the men you described possess such a weapon?'

'Yes, Skinner Grouch wore one in a sheath across his chest.' His hands were raised as he struggled for words to describe the knife, but Trusk produced the blade in question and cut him short.

Rusty gripped the bars of his cell. 'He actually left his knife in the body?'

Trusk nodded. 'That surprise you?'

Rusty nodded in his turn. 'When you

play with people for a long time you begin to get ideas about them. I would have said that Skinner had killed with that weapon many times before. I would have thought he would have taken it with him.'

'That would have been *my* idea, too,' Trusk admitted.

'Are you plannin' on goin' up that gully after the killers, marshall?' Rusty wanted to know.

Trusk half closed his eyes and stared at Waters, who was shifting his feet uneasily on the far side of the desk.

'What makes you think *I* don't suspect you of the killin', young fellow?'

The marshal's question was put bluntly. It was intended to disconcert a young man feeling over-confident. Rusty merely raised his brows. His confidence had been building up ever since the marshal started to listen to him.

'Oh, I don't know, marshal. There'll be folks around who could testify that I was sleepin' on a bench outside the saloon long before the others pulled out of the back room.'

Waters looked doubtful, as if he was about to argue about the suggestions, but Rusty went on.

'Like the old fellow in the tattered poncho who occupied the bench before I did, an' that tired-lookin' barman who served me with beer . . . on my own.'

Rusty paused for breath, and this time Waters had nothing to say. It was time for a show of initiative on the part of the prisoner.

'Now see here, marshal, I've lost money to the men you seek. Moreover, I've been cheated. Why don't you let me out of here? I'll lead a bunch of riders after them up that gully, although I'm quite sure there are snags which might deter an ordinary local man.'

Trusk flickered his jutting brows. He did not look in the cell direction but, obviously, he was interested in the offer and in his deputy's reaction to it.

Waters pointed a finger at Rusty. 'He's jest usin' this suggestion as a way to go free, marshal. How do we know he ain't in cahoots with the others?'

The marshal played around with the stacked cards. After a while, he suggested: 'We could put him in the lead. If they're waitin' for us along the gully, he'd be the first to feel the flyin' lead.'

Waters snorted. Rusty sighed. The latter spoke. 'All right, put me up in front. I'll take a chance on bein' ambushed, if it will make you take me on trust. I'll do it any way you suggest.'

Waters then argued without conviction. Trusk approved Rusty's offer. Waters' cronies were dispersed, and the marshal harangued those townsmen who were still hanging about outside and craving for action. He talked with the murder weapon in his fist, explained that the stranger in custody had been an innocent victim of the cheating gamblers and that he was willing to lead a posse up Rustlers' Gully in pursuit.

A bit of swift repartee convinced all the dissident ones that the peace officer knew what he was talking about, and presently the crowd thinned out, leaving a dozen men who were willing to ride, almost immediately, in the wake of the killers.

★  ★  ★

Deputy Waters, secretly far from keen on having any part of the expedition, nevertheless went along in charge, prompted by his ambition to take over the marshal's job. In the first fifteen minutes, he had very little to say to Rusty, but as the gully deepened and widened into a ravine of some magnitude, the dark-haired young man on the dappled grey horse eased back alongside of the deputy's buckskin and insisted upon an exchange of views.

'Now, look here, Waters, you know this route a whole lot better than *I* do. You don't like me because I handled you roughly, earlier on, but if I get picked off by the jaspers supposed to be up ahead of us, *you*'ll be the second man in their gun sights. So tell me about this gully an' where it leads.'

'You're lookin' for an excuse to get out of the job of scout,' Waters scoffed as he massaged his magnificent growth of moustache.

'If you don't co-operate, I don't lead any more, friend. So please yourself.'

Rusty went through the motions of checking his horse and dropping further back to join the main body of riders. He had had his weapons restored to him as well as his confidence.

'Hold it,' Waters ordered reluctantly. 'All right, I'll tell you what I know.'

The deputy spoke slowly and with care. Soon the animosity died between them and Rusty found himself visualizing the interesting and formidable terrain ahead of them. Rustlers' Gully was so named because it had been used in the past by men stealing cattle from the ranches in and around Prairie City who wanted a bolt hole out of the district.

Within a mile or two, the gully changed into a ravine, which then broadened into a stone-strewn valley floor pitted with rock and tangled with gorse-like scrub guaranteed to deter all but the very determined. The general direction was west varying at times to south-west. After a ride of an hour or two the quality of the terrain so deteriorated that the area could very well have been referred to as Bad Lands.

A snaking narrow track headed generally westward towards the border with New Mexico territory while the tired-looking pockmarked valley finally fragmented into the mouths of three canyons. Rumour had it among the towns of the area that one, and probably two of the canyons were boxes.

Anyone uninformed beforehand, therefore, would be taking a considerable gamble if they entered the canyons with the hope of riding on through, still ahead of determined pursuit.

Rusty discussed all that Waters told him and then asked questions of his own. 'Are we likely to run across the mouths of these canyons tonight, in daylight?'

Waters shook his head. 'To tell you the truth I've never made this run before. Judgin' by what I've heard in the past, I'd say we are not makin' enough speed to see the canyons' mouths today. I could ask for a greater effort, but it wouldn't be rightly fair, would it?'

The deputy gestured around at the concealing rocks, near and far, any number of which could have successfully concealed gunmen bent on decimating a small posse limited to fourteen in over-all numbers.

'Do you think they'll attack us if we press them close?'

Waters worked on his jaw and neck with his bandanna. He shrugged. 'Surely you could answer that better than I could. It depends upon how aggressive they are, an' how they feel about attackin' men in numbers.'

'I think they are united and ruthless enough to attack your party, an' they'd do it from an ambush. From stealth.'

'Any suggestions?' Waters asked.

'If you won't think I'm trying to deceive you,' Rusty replied tentatively. 'Give your boys a break for coffee, then ask for more speed. Me, I'll jest rock my saddle an' push on ahead. If I see or hear anything I'll get word to you. Will that be all right?'

Waters nodded. 'I guess it will have to be.' For the first time, he smiled at the man he had earlier locked up. Rusty reflected that it had been a very busy day, and that it was still far from finished.

\* \* \*

For two hours after he parted from the other riders, Rusty pushed on. He was very much on the alert because he had no wish to become a victim of the men he sought. Dusty earth, complicated by small rock, occasional clumps of cactus, pot-holes and straggling lengths of thorny scrub reduced his rate of progress very appreciably. He was determined, if he could, to get within viewing distance of the canyon mouths before the sun dipped in the west.

★　★　★

He worked his spyglass frequently in the last hour before sunset. As the yawning canyon entrances came nearer, the light gradually faded. Sign on the trail was almost non-existent and exceedingly difficult to identify. Reason suggested that the fugitives would take the trail over the border rather than risk riding into a box.

The plodding grey moved on towards the west, where the setting orange disc of light was gradually being cut off at the bottom by the horizon. In the gathering gloom, the three canyon mouths to the south merged into one. Suddenly the sun was gone. The eyes stopped straining. In place of light was the tricky inky blackness of night.

Occasionally, the grey's shoes struck sparks off the trail, but no probing gun shots sought to empty the saddle. Rusty pushed on for another ten minutes. When the grey stumbled sufficiently badly to have injured itself, he called a halt and grimly checked it over for sprains. Fortunately, there were none.

The rider was tired. His best concentration was behind him.

# 3

Trail discipline made the lone rider give attention to his tired mount before his own needs. Feeling fairly convinced that he had neither friend nor foe anywhere near him, he stripped off his bed-roll, saddle and blanket and allowed the over-heated grey to wander in search of food.

There was no running water near at hand, and the straggle of grass which the foraging animal turned up was brown, withered and scarcely edible. Rusty said as much to the stallion and the empty world at large. He plucked a few handfuls of the scant fodder and used it to roughly groom his mount. His efforts evoked no special response, and it was only when he took off his hat and poured about a third of the contents of his water canteen into it that the grey snickered in appreciation.

While the uncertain business of drinking from the hat trough was going on, Rusty became aware of extra sounds. In the oppressive silence of the wilderness he could hear the distant jingle of harness coming down the trail which he had already used.

He frowned and showed surprise that Waters and his riders were still on the move. What did they hope to achieve by pushing on after nightfall? Had the deputy some special scheme in mind, or was he merely seeking to create a determined image in his posse riders' minds?

Rusty decided that Waters was quite shrewd in some things, and in others rather ill advised. Having dealt with his mount, he took a drink himself and rather leisurely gathered wood for a fire. All the time he was busy, screwing up his eyes to defeat the almost total darkness, he was listening for developments as the larger group approached. He finished building his fire and arranged his saddle and blanket at what he thought was the most desirable angle to it, and then hesitated over putting a light to the wood.

Something was puzzling him. The horse and harness sounds were no longer coming from the expected direction. As near as he could judge in the dark, the party had left the ill-defined trail and ridden roughly in the direction of the nearest canyon mouth. He recalled Waters having said that he had never ridden in this direction before, and he wondered if the deputy had blundered off the trail or taken advice from some of his fellow riders.

Rusty toyed with his revolver, wondering if Waters would get back on trail in answer to a gunfire signal. Uncertainty made him re-holster his gun and wait.

'All right, all right, so I heard you!'

The disgruntled voice was that of Waters, acknowledging a second shout from further back, telling him that he had gone off the trail.

The deputy added: 'Rein in an' dismount right where you are, boys! You should have shouted earlier. All this ridin' in semi-darkness lulled me into sleep.'

Tired and irritable, the deputy backtracked to the spot where his equally tired supporters were swinging out of leather and cursing the fugitives and the devilishly difficult terrain. Having admitted to a moment of weakness, Waters hastened to get his men organized. Three of the men who were skilled with horses took over the handling of all the animals while the rest set about raising a fire and preparing supplies for an evening meal. The general feeling of the posse members was that they were well and truly out of touch with the fugitives and that they should make the best of a bad job.

The fire flared into life within five minutes. Several coffee pots appeared, suspended on a horizontal wooden pole over forked sticks planted vertically in the ground. One or two of the relaxing horses frisked around wide of the aura of firelight, kicking up their hind legs and generally making happy noises as the gear was stripped off them.

Six or seven men were moving against the brilliant light of the crackling fire when the sudden crackle of rifle fire came from the intense blackness to the south. Startled shouts and oaths filled the air as the flying lead ripped into their midst. A coffee pot was ventilated. Flaming branches and sparks flew out of the fire. More serious, two of the moving men were hit and sank to the ground before the party took obvious avoiding action.

'Down! Down everybody! Take cover, an' bring up the rifles!'

The first fusillade died down, and all the defenders by the fire were looking in the obvious direction as the attacking guns briefly lanced flame again. This time there was only one cry, more in anger than in pain. About ten guns retaliated and the exchanges became general.

'Spread out! Keep clear of the fire, an' watch out for crawlin' men!'

Waters' hoarse voice was unmistakable to anyone who knew him. It carried to Rusty Redman who had still not put a match to his fire. The latter was whistling soundlessly to himself as he gathered his Winchester and a pouchful of shells. Rusty felt that he had been more than passing lucky not to have been ambushed earlier himself by the hostile group now known to be bellied down nearer the canyon mouth.

Clearly, the blundering off the trail by the posse had been a piece of ill-timed luck. If they had not suffered casualties, they were lucky. Perhaps Rusty's intervention might turn their luck and prevent future losses on the side of law and order, if he used the element of surprise judiciously.

The rifle exchanges continued. Here and there, brief flashes indicated that men on the flank of the renegade line were moving closer in an effort to catch one or two deputies unawares.

Minus his spurs, and moving as quietly as possible, Rusty moved a good fifty yards nearer the hostile positions. He began to feel that he could wait too long, in the event that Malone and Grouch decided to pull out and change their position in the darkness.

Someone by the fire snatched a burning brand out of it and hurled it some distance towards the attackers. This piece of opportunism provoked a lot of return shooting which Rusty used to good advantage. Firing from a standing position, he pumped shells at three of the flashes, levering as rapidly as he could. The other bullets in his magazine were fired at random in between the known positions.

As he dropped flat with his ears reacting to the sudden cracks from his weapon, Rusty listened. Mixed with the cries of consternation were two other yells, which suggested that he might have winged one man or more.

No sooner had he hit the ground than the loner scuttled away down-trail. A positive fusillade of bullets homed into the earth or whistled over it where he had been standing. The nearest one to a hit was a chance shot off the target area which kicked up dust and small stones under his nose as he moved.

There was a pause in the shooting from around the fire as they adjusted to the new situation. After a short pause, they fired spasmodically. In answer to return fire, Rusty got off a telling shot or two and then moved on again.

The young man remained watchful in case the renegades decided to make a concerted move against him. Some thirty minutes later, he tired of his efforts at finding targets in the darkness and the exchanges between the two groups faded to nothing.

Gradually, the fire settled down. The weaving shadows which came from it occasionally illuminated a ghostly moving horse, but no humans moved against it. Night pinned down the dour contestants like a cool blanket.

As the sky turned to dark grey and gradually lightened, Rusty was asleep behind a convenient rock with his cheek pushed into the crown of his stetson and his cold Winchester still to hand.

Already men were covertly moving near the dead fire, and a sharp call from that direction alerted the sleeper, who blinked himself awake, squirmed over into a prone position and started to peer around him. In the direction of the canyon mouth, the visibility was still too obscure for useful observation.

He was reasonably sure that none of the enemy were close at hand. His brow furrowed as he peered around and failed to locate his mount. He decided that it could not be too far away and that the time was ripe to make closer contact with the main group.

He cupped his hands to his mouth and shouted.

'Ho, there, Waters, are you all right?'

A few seconds elapsed before the familiar hoarse voice replied cautiously.

'That you, Redman? If it is, come on over! We think the other group has pulled out, but we can't be sure. Be careful, you hear me?'

'I hear you, friend! I'm comin' over!'

Rusty crawled twenty yards before one of the furthest deputies from the defensive ring spotted him and hailed him from close-up.

'We're still keeping a lookout, but we figure they withdrew after you hit them on the flank! We were lucky you showed up when you did!'

'Any casualties?'

'Yes, one man dead and another wounded in the shoulder. We didn't come out of the exchange too well.'

'Any plans for today?'

'You'd best get in by the fire an' talk to Kyle. He's jest gettin' the boys together with the intention of makin' plans.'

Behind a sizeable boulder, Rusty shook hands with the man who had greeted him. Five minutes later, when the state of the light had vastly improved, Rusty was surrounded by the tired riders, most of whom had attempted to keep awake all night to offset another possible sneak attack.

While they were commiserating with one another, a man who had seen service as a scout with the army came in from a long crawling reconnaissance. His hat came off his head and he grinned wolfishly as he recognized the newcomer.

He remarked: 'The opposition have definitely pulled out. I, for one, didn't hear any sounds as they pulled out. I thought the horses might have given them away. If you want my guess they've definitely headed into the canyons. Probably the first.'

The scout, whose name was Royce, raised his sharply arched brows at Rusty, who gave his opinion. 'I fell asleep towards dawn, but I'd swear they didn't go past me on the trail. My guess would be the same, that they went into the first canyon. You should be able to check that by sign, if you intend to follow them up.'

Deputy Waters nodded and scowled. He slowly lowered his weight on to a rock, while some of his men boosted the fire and flapped their arms to restore circulation. While the leader stared at the corpse, respectfully covered by a blanket, the rest awaited his opinion.

'I'll have to give our forward policy some thought. In any case, ain't nothin' goin' to happen till we've taken breakfast. Go fetch your mount, Redman. You'll be wantin' to join us for a proper meal.'

Rusty grinned wearily at him, nodded to the others and went off in search of the grey, leaving his Winchester behind. By the time he got back, the talk was about two dead outlaws. Malone and Grouch had left their dead behind them. Their numbers were reduced to four, and they had declined to do the honourable thing by their deceased comrades in case they were overtaken by superior numbers.

Stacey, the wounded man, had his arm in a sling. He was a bulky, bearded, determined farmer, who did not intend to let his wound interfere with the posse's plans. Rusty met him by the fire, where he was frying bacon in a skillet. After taking food from him, the dark-haired young man struck up a conversation.

'I'm sorry about your shoulder. You'll need to go back to town with that, whatever Waters decides to do for the future.'

Stacey nodded heavily. 'But I won't need any escort. In fact, I can manage my horse and lead Jan Gorse's animal as well. Gorse is the man who was killed. What'll you be doin'?'

'I don't rightly know for sure,' Rusty admitted, as he nibbled the bacon. 'It all depends if Waters thinks I'm still indebted to the town. I'm on my way to Redman City, New Mexico, which is a good long haul from here.'

Stacey sniffed hard and gave away the last of the bacon to a late-comer. 'If you ask me, the town never did have any hold on you. You did your bit last night, when you hit those jaspers on the flank. You don't owe us anything. Tell Waters I said so, an' pull out as soon as you can.'

Some men were still eating on their feet when the group came together to discuss their future movements. Stacey had warmed to Rusty, and he opened the discussion with his own suggestions.

'Kyle, I'll be headed back to town takin' poor old Jan Gorse with me pretty soon. Redman, here, has a long trip ahead of him. All the way to Redman City, New Mexico. What'll you do? Are you headin' into the canyon or givin' up the chase?'

Waters cleared his throat. 'We're beholden to Redman for what he did last night. He's free to go as soon as he pleases. As for the rest of us, I think we'll spend one more day on this chase. The odds are probably two to one against the runaways gettin' clear through that canyon. They're reduced in numbers an' we may be lucky. I hope so. I don't like casualties on my side.'

The meal was soon finished. Camp was broken. Waters and his fit men headed straight for the canyon mouth, leaving Rusty to tidy up and see Stacey on his way with the led horse. Just before the wounded man was boosted into the saddle prior to departure for Prairie City, the talk turned to Redman City.

'If you ain't been there before, young fellow, you may be in for a surprise or two.'

Rusty raised his brows, deeply interested in the new topic.

'Folks do say that Redman City is run mostly for the Redmans and those who do things *their* way. Folks who don't hit it off with the Redman clan don't do so well. In fact, a lot of them come away altogether, an' few are said to return. So, I hope you won't be too disappointed, amigo.'

Rusty, who was mildly baffled, thanked Stacey for his comments, boosted him into the saddle and saw him off trailing the late Jan Gorse strapped to a second horse. Stacey managed a wave before a bend in the trail finally put Rusty out of sight. The latter appreciated that it was a bit tricky for a man doing all his work with one hand.

As he galloped the grey off down the track which led to the territorial line he had very mixed feelings about the future.

# 4

Still very determined to complete his journey and visit Redman City, Rusty Redman crossed into New Mexico in twenty-four hours without further incident. Gradually, the goings on in and around Prairie City moved to the back of his mind and his thoughts were wholly on the future.

Twice in a week, he paused in small settlements to rest his horse. On other days, he pushed on, making ten to fifteen miles, always moving towards the south-west where that formidable river, the Pecos, separated him from the true Redman country.

The town of South Wells, dusty, sun-drenched and isolated loomed up in front of him on the seventh day. He entered it at a time when he was suffering from trail fatigue and in need of a few distractions at five o'clock in the afternoon.

There were a few strollers about, although the town was far from brisk for the time of the day. Business in the shops was not particularly marked. It was early for the restaurants and bars to start winning the day's customers.

He still had money left from the time when his parents sold out in Wichita and on this occasion, he felt like squandering a few dollars without getting involved, as he had done in Prairie City. About a third of the way up the main street he came across two buildings side by side.

The first was a saloon with the unusual name of the Whisky Bucket. His attention was drawn to it because its imposing frontage stood back behind the fronts of the other buildings by some thirty feet. Jutting out to sidewalk level was a wide, open drinking area overhung by a wooden awning with decorative fringed pelmets. Two parallel wooden tables were placed on the gallery and seated at one of them was an affable fellow of mature years in a grey suit and a straw hat. He was drinking beer from a clay pot and taking an active interest in the comings and goings in the street.

Rusty noted the clearness of his blue eyes and his obvious interest, but he did not acknowledge the observer at first. He slowed the grey which was dust-caked and blowing lightly, and glanced beyond the gallery at the freshly-painted frontage of the Wells Hotel, which looked as if it might charge a fairly high rate for its rooms and service.

'Sure is difficult to know what to do first when a man hits town with the father and mother of a thirst, ain't it, stranger? If you were to ask my advice, I'd say visit the livery first. Try the one up the far end on the left side. There's always a room spare at the hotel. You can book in later. If you get back in five minutes, I'll have a pot of cool beer waiting for you. How would that be?'

Rusty would have found it hard to conceal his interest in any circumstances. He wiped his dry mouth on the sleeve of his shirt, grinned in a way which had been described from time to time as infectious, and removed his hat.

'All right, sir, I accept your offer. My name is Rusty to my friends. What do I call you?'

'Jefferson More, retired businessman, Jeff, if you like. These days I'm gradually puttin' money into the Whisky Bucket an' takin' beer out. I'll be waitin' for you when you get back, Rusty.'

Rusty completed his chore in seven. He found himself looking forward to that beer with a tremendous amount of cheerful anticipation. He had not tasted anything but water since breakfast, and the last lot of beer he had had was definitely sub-standard. Jefferson More moved up the bench, making way for him and pushing forward the pot which he had promised.

Rusty forced a brief show of politeness and then grabbed the pot. He took one look into it, and then drank deeply, swallowing about a third of its contents.

'My word, Jeff, that's a good brew. And cool, too! How do they manage it? What's the secret?'

More chuckled. He undid his waistcoat and massaged his chest, gesturing for Rusty to take more of the beer. 'Aw, it's a private arrangement I have, amigo. When I went out of business I made sure that the proprietor had several big clay pots. Kept in them, the beer stays cool. It *has* to be cool for me, otherwise I'd take my custom elsewhere.'

Rusty accepted a small cigar and only protested mildly when his new friend ordered for the two of them a second time. Presently, the rider's excessive thirst faded and he became talkative.

'Funny how trail ridin' affects you, Jeff. There are times when you feel you'll never live long enough to make the next distant bend. Other times you get the impression you're in between two towns an' you'll stay that way forever. But I'm runnin' on. It's the beer talkin'.'

'Are you a settling man or do you have the urge to keep on travellin' all the time? I ask, because like anybody else in these parts I'm interested in folks who may settle in South Wells.'

Rusty grinned, eyed his cigar and shrugged. 'I don't rightly know, Jeff. I'm not plannin' on stayin' here, but I think I could settle, if the circumstances were right. The fact is, I'm heading for Redman country. My surname is Redman, and I'm goin' to take a look-see at the place, see what it's like. Find out if any of the Redman clan are related to my folks who were living in Kansas until quite recently.

'I don't know a whole lot about Redman City. As a matter of fact, I've heard mixed reports. Maybe you've been there, or heard about the place in your travels.'

This was a plain invitation for the older man to open up. For the first time since their coming together, he looked mildly embarrassed. He lowered his head so that his hat brim shadowed his eyes.

Rusty waited patiently. He was not disappointed.

'Old Man Redman was the fellow they all used to talk about. He must have been a powerful character. They say that somehow or another he managed to keep both warring factions, the Yankees and Confederates off his ranch land all through the war between the North and the South.

'That must have taken some doing. And shortly after the armistice there was a period when law and order wasn't any too good. Armed bands roamed about this part of the west, and it took mighty formidable opposition to stop them. The Redmans held them off, so I believe. I also heard it said that the Redman boys never joined up in either army. But I couldn't say if it were true.

'We don't hear so much about Old Man Redman these days. There's another generation. They seem to have learned a lot from him. Redman City is what its name suggests, a city run for and by the Redmans. Anyone who doesn't hit it off with them doesn't ever amount to much. If you take my advice, you'll go along there with an open mind. If you don't like what you see and hear, come away again. Don't be a party to it. The west is a big place. Maybe there's more than one type of Redman in this man's country.'

Rusty had kept nodding. He had a feeling that Jefferson More knew a whole lot more than he had revealed about Redman territory. He wanted to ask probing questions, but something totally unexpected cut across his intentions.

A young, well-dressed and attractive woman was hovering in the foyer of the hotel next door, looking agitated and obviously trying to get the attention of Jefferson More.

Rusty cleared his throat. 'I'd like to have talked a whole lot more, Jeff, but I have a feeling there's a young woman who knows you better than I do, and who needs your attention right now a great deal more than I do. If you like, I'll push off.'

More shrugged off the frown which Redman talk had put on his face, turned and glanced over his shoulder and expressed surprise and pleasure when he recognized the young woman.

'Why, Laura, why didn't you say you were in town?' he protested. 'I had no idea.' He turned to Rusty. 'Finish your beer, Rusty. I'll be right back.'

'Okay, Jeff, go right ahead. I've taken up a lot of your time, anyway.'

Rusty had a good look at the young woman before he turned his back on her and his new found friend and made a big show of rolling himself a cigarette.

Laura was in her middle twenties. She had auburn hair worn long to her shoulders and curled at the ends. A small green bonnet was perched fetchingly on the top of her head. Her green eyes were wide-set and intense. Her forehead was broad; a long elegant neck was encircled by a green velvet band. The dress which showed off her contours was of the same colour. Rusty noted the small dark smudges under her eyes, as if she had not slept well, and a black mourning band around one arm.

The sidewalk in front of the hotel was deserted at the time. More glanced into the hotel foyer, found there was no one about there either and at once engaged the girl in conversation.

'Has anything further happened?' he enquired anxiously.

The girl bit her lip. 'Well, nothing definite, Jeff, but I have the feeling they'll be coming for me. I don't feel safe after what happened to Simeon. It — it was all on account of me that they — they ganged up on him like they did. I have this feeling, I'm absolutely convinced they'll turn up one day and insist that I go back with them. Can you help me?'

Rusty's hearing was particularly acute. He gave no sign that he could hear what they were saying. There was a slight pause before More replied.

'Well, I hope I can, Laura. You know I always have your best interests at heart. But what do you plan to do? Where are you thinking of going? It's clear you won't want to stay in South Wells.'

'I've made up my mind to seek out Jabez, that's Simeon's brother, you know. He has a cabin and a small farm way out in the country, south of here. I thought if I hid myself away for a while, the men who are seeking me will go away and, and leave me in peace. The only thing is, I won't feel safe until I'm clear of the towns. As soon as they know I've quit Northend, they'll come this way lookin' for me. It isn't easy for a young woman to keep her movements a secret, Jeff.'

More sighed heavily. 'But you'll want some sort of an escort to take you to Jabez's home, won't you? You jest can't go out ridin' all on your own. You might get lost on the way, an' that would be almost as bad as bein' taken back.'

'So what do you suggest, Jeff?'

'You could go by coach part of the way. There's a coach through tomorrow. You could keep out of sight until then.'

'Oh, no, no I don't want to spend the night here. You know a lot of people. Couldn't you hunt up somebody who is entirely reliable to go along with me? We could pay a man well, if he was prepared to leave almost at once.'

Clearly, More was baffled. He advised: 'Go to your room, Laura. I have to have time to think, to make some arrangements. If I was twenty years younger I'd be glad to take on the job myself.'

With an obvious show of reluctance, the young woman retired indoors. More tapped with his foot on the steps of the hotel. Eventually he remembered Rusty and he wandered back to renew the acquaintance.

'When I have a problem, I get to feelin' hungry, Rusty. Would you care to take a meal with me?'

'Only if you'll allow me to pay, seein as how you've bought all the beer so far.'

With a sigh and a grin, the older man agreed to the arrangement. He led the way to a café which he used for most of his meals and, in a curtained alcove, he ordered for both of them. Half way through the beef course, Rusty thought that the silence ought to be broken.

'If I can help you with that young woman's problem, don't hesitate to ask. I know where I want to go, I'm not expected by anyone. That's to say I can take time out if I want it.'

More nodded and ate more food before opening up. 'Laura Burke is a widow.'

Rusty whistled but offered no comment.

'Her husband, Simeon, was manoeuvred into a fatal shooting incident by a trio of men hired by the girl's family who did not approve of her marriage. The shooting occurred only ten days ago. She and her husband were managing a shop which was started with some capital advanced by me. It was in the next town further north, known as Northend.

'Right now, she has this strong feeling that her family's hirelings will appear one day soon and take her back to where she started from. Believe me, she has no desire to go back, and she's right. Some folks would say she married jest to get away from her kin. I wouldn't know about that.'

'Is she lookin' for a protector?' Rusty prompted.

More raised his brows. He began to realize that Rusty had heard something of what they had been saying earlier. 'She needs a guide and a guard, jest for a short period. The job would be over in a couple of days and then you'd be free to go wherever you want to go. There's one snag. She wants to start almost straight away.'

Rusty pushed away his plate with a sigh of satisfaction.

'Well, I haven't booked in yet. I'll

take the job on. It seems kind of odd, though. I mean she'll be takin' a chance with a stranger like me. You will be, too. I wonder how good a judge of character you are, Jeff.'

'We'll both be gamblin' on you, Rusty. And I hope I've judged you right. As soon as we've finished this meal I'll take you along to see her.'

In spite of the fact that he had planned to idle his time away in South Wells for a day or two, Rusty was excited about the prospect of leaving again on a secret mission with a girl in distress. The prospect pleased him. He found his mind going back over the few books he had been fortunate enough to read.

Somewhere, he had come across an unusual observation. 'It is sometimes better to travel hopefully than to arrive.' He wondered if this applied to his own present circumstances. In any case, Redman City could wait for a day or two longer.

# 5

Scarcely two hours had gone by since Rusty arrived in South Wells when the trio got together in a private lounge at the hotel for the discussion. Laura was the last to arrive. She slipped in unobserved and surprised both More and Rusty by her change of appearance.

Gone were the elegant dress and bonnet. In their place was a neatly tailored horse riding outfit which appreciably changed the widow's appearance. Her hair was tied back at the nape of the neck in a green ribbon. On her head was a flat-crowned cream stetson. Her bandanna was the same colour. A grey man's shirt with twin pockets partially masked her femininity. A new pair of denims did the rest.

More stood up and pushed a padded chair towards her.

'Sit down, Laura. This is a young

66

man who is prepared to help you. His name is Rusty. He's on a long journey, but he's prepared to take a day or two to see you to your destination before he moves on. Point is, do you think the two of you can get along together?'

'Howdy, Rusty, I'm pleased to meet you.'

'That goes for me, too, Laura.' Having removed his hat as soon as the girl entered the room, Rusty now moved across to her and shook hands. 'You don't need to go into any details about your troubles. I'll be glad to escort you wherever you want to go. Do you think I'd be suitable as an escort?'

Laura coloured up a little. She shifted her position and shot a fleeting glance at the older man. 'If Jeff has confidence in you, then I'm certainly satisfied. Are you sure it won't inconvenience you too much if we leave almost immediately?'

'I had planned to spend a day or two here in South Wells, but it doesn't matter. I can come back again when this little job is over, if I feel like it. If you're agreeable, I think we ought to do a little plannin', don't you? Think about eatables on the way, an' that sort of thing.'

More butted in. 'All right, so it's settled. You two get to know each other a little better while I collect your horses and the victuals you were talking about.' Jeff rose to his feet, touched his hat to Laura and backed out.

Suddenly Rusty was short of things to say. He shifted uneasily this way and that, and finally excused himself for a short while, saying that he had to get under a pump before escorting a lady. He had just arrived back, shaved and in a new shirt when a boy messenger arrived from More.

'Mr More said for you two to walk through to South Street an' meet him at the east end. Is that all right?'

Rusty nodded and tossed the boy a two-bit piece, assisted Laura to her feet, and left the building without further loss of time. The grey stallion had been well groomed. So had the black mare which was to be the girl's riding horse. More chatted with them briefly in the shade of a clump of trees before boosting the girl into the saddle and wishing them luck.

In a little more than a hundred yards they were clear of the town and some of the tension was going out of the girl.

'No one in particular seems to have observed our departure,' Rusty remarked. 'I guess it will be all right if we take a leisurely pace.'

Laura, jogging along beside him, laughed nervously. 'I don't want to be a nuisance to you, Rusty, but I'll feel better if we didn't ride too slowly in the first hour or so. I know the route, so we shan't have any troubles along those lines. In fact, it may sound strange, but I'd rather be lost than found.'

Some four hundred yards further on, a lesser track diverged from the main one used by regular horse and wheeled vehicle traffic. Laura glanced either way up the main route, and headed the mare on to the secondary trail without hesitation.

After that, she led the way at a useful speed for upwards of two hours. Clearly, the track they were using had scarcely ever accommodated wheeled vehicles. There had been horses, and they, if Rusty was any judge of such things, had been few and far between.

While they were slaking their thirst from canteens, Rusty remarked: 'Laura, there can't be more than a half hour of daylight left. I think we ought to look for a camping site, right away.'

The girl wrestled with near panic, succeeded in getting her nerves under control, and agreed. 'There ought to be some runnin' water somewhere around. I can't think which direction to take.'

'How would it be if I take over, then?'

Laura swallowed hard and awaited instructions. She began to have a feeling of guilt through not having asked his advice before. While he studied the semi-luxurious landscape through his spyglass, she felt sure that the darkness was creeping in upon them.

'We'll have to gamble,' Rusty murmured. 'Down there, to our left, I'd say. On that lower ground through those trees. I think I can see a willow or two, but the water — if it's there — must be slow movin'. I can't hear anything but the rustle of foliage.'

They took Rusty's proposed route and when he found a narrow slow-moving stream within two hundred yards, Laura warmed to him. The saddles were slackened and the horses given a chance to wade in and drink. Further upstream, the riders did the same, cooling their bootless feet and gradually relaxing.

'We're far enough from anywhere to have a fire and a few home comforts,' Rusty observed, as he waded ashore. 'Take a look in the saddle pockets, why don't you, while I gather some fire-wood?'

Laura nodded and hurried to do his bidding. The fire blossomed and formed a pleasing aura as the inky blackness of night descended upon them. The girl prepared a meal of bacon and flapjacks, which they washed down with a good brew of coffee. She also rolled cigarettes for him, and tentatively offered him a light with a burning twig.

He wondered if her attentions were prompted by breeding, or whether she was fussing him because she felt beholden to him. Their bed-rolls were laid out on either side of the fire. For a long time they felt shy of wishing one another good night.

Rusty checked over his weapons when he thought his companion was asleep, but she roused herself with a sudden start and whispered her 'good night' greetings. After that, her breathing became deeper and she drifted off into a deep sleep.

Rusty, mindful that he was really the guard, slept fitfully. On one occasion, he heard her sobbing in her sleep and was reminded that she had lost her husband in the recent past in harrowing circumstances. Shortly after dawn, his unsatisfactory night made him restless. He determined to revive himself with an early bathe. Gathering up his discarded clothes, he catfooted upstream. Some fifty yards away he stripped off completely and stretched out in the shallow, allowing the cool refreshing waters to run over him.

He was towelling himself briskly on the bank when he thought he heard a faint cry from the direction of the camp. He listened hard, and presently came the sounds of furtive movement through the scrub back from the bank.

'Laura, is that you?'

She gasped, and he moved up the bank a few yards, discovering her directly behind him with a revolver wobbling in her hand.

'What is it, Laura?' he questioned brusquely. 'Somebody comin'?'

The girl lowered her gun hand. 'No. I'm sorry, Rusty. I thought you'd gone, that's all. I thought you'd slipped away in the night.'

He slipped behind a tree bole and manfully hauled up his trousers. Presently, the humour of the situation got through to him.

'All's well, then. I slept more or less with one eye open. Then I thought I'd freshen up with a bathe before breakfast. You could do the same, if you felt like it.'

Sighing with relief, Laura turned her head. 'I don't think I will, after all. I'll work on the fire, and then maybe take a wash. You don't need to hurry, now I know you're here an' everything's all right.'

They ate more or less in silence. Talk of their route inevitably followed. When Rusty complimented her upon her sense of direction, Laura produced a pencilled map of the way to Jabez Burke's shack and between them they figured out the distance to be covered.

Half an hour later, they had the

mounts saddled and were ready to depart.

'What sort of a man is your brother-in-law?'

'Something of a loner, I guess, Rusty. He's spent some time in the army. Now, he lives on his own. He does a little farming, and shooting and fishing. There was a strong bond between my husband and Jabez, although the one we're goin' to see isn't the marryin' kind.'

'Did he come to the funeral?'

'He was late for the burial, but he paid his respects to me later and insisted that I came to his place if I needed any help at all. We should see him, all being well, around noon.'

The rest of the journey was over bumpy, scarcely-broken ground. It was after one o'clock in the afternoon before they located the east-west valley from a high point about half a mile to the north-east. Rusty studied the wooded vale through his glass and then handed it to Laura, who squinted through it with great interest.

'Are you sure that's the place, Laura?' he asked tentatively. 'There's not much sign of life down there.'

'That's it, all right, Rusty. The shack is through the trees up the west end of the draw. There's a nice little stream on the low side of it, too, although you wouldn't think it from up here.'

Kneeing the mare nearer to the grey, she handed back the spyglass. Her hand trembled and she almost dropped it on the ground.

'Why, what's the trouble, Laura?'

'I, er, I've got the jitters again. Your job is nearly over, Rusty. And I've felt so secure with you around. Except for that incident when I thought you'd pulled out. Maybe I'm feelin' nervous because you'll be on your way again soon.'

Rusty was a little baffled by the state Laura was in. He was flattered by her suggestion that his presence made her feel safe, but he wondered how she really felt about her brother-in-law:

whether he would give her the same sort of secure feeling.

'How would if be if I rode on down ahead of you, sort of spied out the land? Would that make you feel better?'

'Oh, well, yes, indeed, Rusty. If it wouldn't be too much trouble. You see, I may have to spend some time there, and I have to feel sure about it from the start.'

'Don't give it another thought,' he replied, with his broadest grin. 'Jest dismount for a while and take the weight off your legs. Don't do anything at all until you have a definite signal from me. Feelin' like you do, I'd keep out of sight an' not do anything to attract attention to myself. Okay?'

Rusty thought she looked good when the confidence was in her. He feasted his eyes on her animated face before riding off down the gentle slope, a dark young man, tall in the saddle. A lady's protector, and proud of it.

★ ★ ★

Jabez Burke's shack was a peeled-log cabin with a door back and front and a window in each wall. In the last hundred yards, Rusty began to see signs which suggested that it was in use. There were hens and a cow or two in a fenced-off patch wide of one end, bales of hay here and there and a kitchen garden.

Amid the trees on the near side, there was a neat stack of short sawn logs for fuel, but the chimney lacked smoke and there were no immediate signs of any riding stock near the building. Rusty whistled and jingled his harness to make sure that anyone a little hard of hearing was aware of his arrival, but no one showed and he was clear of the trees and within ten yards of the house when he reined in and dismounted.

At that point he felt a small modicum of Laura's uncertainty. She had never at any time given the impression that Jabez would be away from home. Of course, a man living out in the wilds like this could very well be down the stream fishing or following up some other time-consuming occupation, but Rusty felt himself tensing up.

He felt fleetingly that he might be walking into some sort of a trap, although he could not have explained why.

He called sharply: 'Jabez! Jabez Burke, are you there?'

No answer. Not even an echo. Rusty pulled off his stetson, tugged up his white bandanna and nervously wiped his forehead where the short blue-black hair was flattened. He went forward cautiously, his .45 Colt to hand and hesitated by the door. It was closed, but not locked. He knocked, waited again, called out once more and finally opened up and went in.

Emptiness. No sense of staleness as though it had been shut up and left. No humans about, that was all. He studied the two-tier wooden bunks against one wall, the home-made table and chairs and glanced up into the open-ended loft. A single man's belongings here and there, but no man. No Jabez Burke.

For the first time, Rusty wondered what he would have to do with Laura if the man they had come to see did not show up at all. *There* was a problem!

He glanced briefly through a window on the far side, failed to see any signs of the owner and was about to make his way out by the same door when the unexpected happened. The rear door opened without noise and a voice said: 'Raise your hands real slow, stranger, an' explain your presence!'

Rusty had already holstered his revolver. He hoisted his hands. The short hairs at the nape of his neck were prickling, and yet he kept telling himself that the picture did not have to be as black as his startled imagination painted it.

'I'm jest a fellow out of South Wells, who took on a job from Jefferson More. Had to locate a certain Jabez Burke for a lady.'

He was permitted to turn around. Facing him was a man of thirty-five, with dark probing eyes and hollow cheeks, dressed in a Yankee cavalryman's hat and tunic, long since faded. The levis were newer, but they seemed out of keeping with the other clothing.

'What was the lady's name?'

The gun was lowered to the table top, between them.

'Can you prove you are Jabez Burke?'

'This is my cabin, my gun, everything here is mine, an' I'm expectin' trouble from another source, so talk fast, eh? I'll take you on trust, I guess. You definitely ain't one of that murderin' Redman scum, and that's for sure!'

Rusty flinched and was about to protest, but something in Burke's manner made him change his mind. 'Your sister-in-law, Laura, wanted to come and join you with the minimum of delay. I volunteered to bring her.'

Burke whistled. 'Laura's *here*? In the valley?'

Rusty nodded. 'What's the trouble?'

'I've been expectin' her all right, but she could not have come at a worse time. Those darned Redman hirelings have had this cabin under observation since daybreak. They'll be along here at any time.'

He pointed over his shoulder with his thumb, in the opposite direction from which Rusty had approached. Suddenly a new thought occurred to Burke. He paused and nibbled his under lip.

'All this time I've been thinkin' my brother's killers have been wantin' my scalp next. Now, I'm not so sure, maybe they wanted Laura more than me. Maybe they thought findin' me would lead them to her. Does that make sense?'

Rusty shrugged, feeling baffled about all this talk about Redman killers. 'It could be the way you say. But they don't have to get their hands on her. I told her to keep out of sight. She's about half a mile away on high ground, an' she'll stay put until I make contact with her.'

Burke chuckled, his confidence restored. 'That being so, here's a chance for you to extend More's indebtedness to you by strikin' a blow against Laura's and my enemies. What do you say?'

The dark young man had a feeling that everything about the cabin and Burke was unreal, but nevertheless, he contrived to nod.

# 6

First of all, Burke handed over his spyglass and indicated the direction in which Rusty was to look. He trained the glass through a window on the rear side. Scattered across the sloping valley a few hundred yards away were three stands of timber. There was movement in the middle section of trees. A horse's tail twitched, two men, leaning against a tree bole, were talking animatedly and occasionally looking towards the cabin.

'How many men are there?'

'At least four,' Burke replied promptly. 'Probably one of them is a true Redman and the other are hired guns. They mean business. And so do I! The way I read it, they'll be along here in a few minutes. I want you to go and collect my horse and mule. They're over towards the stream, all ready loaded for travel.'

'You're intendin' to pull out?' Rusty queried, as he collapsed the spyglass.

Burke nodded. 'On my own terms, however.'

Rusty wondered what scheme he had in mind, but he was given exact details where to find the animals, and his host ushered him off without giving time for further questions. The younger man found the pinto and the mule without difficulty. He mopped perspiration from his brow, face and neck and slowly massaged his rounded nose before mounting up on the unfamiliar horse and cantering back again.

He sent the two-coloured horse round the end of the cabin and reined in hurriedly as he came in sight of the shack's owner. Burke was busy with a rake, conscientiously moving along a line between the front door of the building and a small bale of hay located among the trees through which Rusty had first approached. The latter dismounted and watched. Burke, knowing he was observed, chuckled grimly to himself. He lifted his soldiering hat, wiped perspiration from his brow and replaced it.

'Those boys sure as hell are due for a hot reception, amigo! What did you say your name was?'

At this juncture nothing would have made Rusty reveal his surname to a man so obviously hostile to the name of Redman. In a little while it would become clear whether Burke was justified in feeling the way he did.

'I didn't. Most folks call me Rusty. Short for Russell. What's that you've got buried?'

'Fuse wire. Go back indoors. Collect anything you think is of value between towns an' get out again as soon as you can. When those jaspers come along here I want us both back in the trees, well clear of the building. Hurry it up, will you?'

Rusty went away without comment. As he hastily gathered up a few items of cutlery, a waistcoat and a couple of boxes of bullets he kept glancing first through one window and then through the other. The group in the trees were just emerging. On the other side, Burke was going through the same routine again, raking from the door to the hay. Rusty was fast gaining the impression that Burke was a very ruthless and determined man, no doubt maintaining his outlook on account of the murder of his brother. It was understandable.

Fuse wire usually meant an explosive. Explosives. The interlopers were due for the most violent sort of reception that a single man's ingenuity could devise.

*   *   *

The intruders were becoming impatient. Their leader, a tall flat-featured character with eroded grey eyes, had been asleep. The laughter of his underlings had aroused him and reminded him of the nearness of a pleasant little creek suitable for bathing.

He leaned over on an elbow. 'Hey, you two! Arkensaw an' Sundown!

What's goin' on by the cottage that's so funny? Answer me straight, I'm gettin' impatient!'

The laughter ceased at once. 'Why, nothin', Vic. Nothin' at all. Sundown, here, thought he saw a face at the window a short while ago, but that's all.'

Arkensaw, a long stooping bandy-legged individual with a nose and chin like Mr Punch, was wary of the leader's hair-trigger temper. He glared at Sundown, hoping that he would say something to placate the boss.

Sundown was a stocky, full-figured man, all of forty years, with a promising jowl and a ready wit, when he was not fearful to use it.

He added: 'All I can say, Vic, is the face at the window wasn't that of no woman. So are you plannin' to change your plans? You said to wait till the girl showed up.'

The fourth man, Reaver, a short red-faced individual, who had been resting nearer the water with a tree supporting his back, turned to listen for the reply.

'Yer, I'm changin' our plans. We could wait here for a week an' she still might not turn up. I don't think this Burke knows where she is anyways. So let's go along there and chat him up a bit. After all, we need a bit of sport. Besides, it ain't much fun hangin' around here if we ain't bathin' or somethin'. So let's go. Saddle up an' let's go talk to the gent.'

Reaver, the shortest of the group, acted as Vic Redman's personal servant. He started to grin as soon as he had something positive to do for the leader. As he worked at rigging the blanket and saddlery on the big skewbald horse perspiration glistened among the black stubble on his chin and upper lip. He did everything except boost the leader into the saddle.

When he was mounted up himself and ready to ride off, he remarked: 'Gosh, Vic, life sure is excitin' since you got yourself into the inner circle of

Redmans. A man knows where he's goin' workin' for a boss like you!'

Arkensaw and Sundown would have liked to mock the short man, but they did not dare because they feared their boss's reaction. Presently, they were on their way, trying to look like everyday travellers and not the predators they really were. Vic Redman had given them one instruction on the short ride. 'Act friendly, at first. Take your cues from me. Me, I'm goin' to play it off the cuff.'

\* \* \*

After making sure that Rusty would back him up, Jabez Burke had settled in hiding among the trees with his weapons to hand. He did not have long to wait. The quartet dismounted a few yards behind the cabin and sauntered cautiously towards the back door.

Someone knocked and received no answer. After a pause, the door was opened and the four men wandered inside. A face appeared at a window in the front wall. Another one replaced it. There was a short conference indoors before the front door was thrown open by a man who kept out of sight.

The leader shouted through the opening. 'Hey, Burke, can you hear me? This is Vic Redman talkin'. I know you're about there somewheres, an' I want to talk to you. Why are you hidin' yourself away?'

Burke and Rusty were some twenty yards apart, hidden behind bulky tree boles. The former soldier leaned out and winked broadly at his partner.

Vic Redman peered through the door. He then stepped through it, took a long look into the trees, failed to notice the two horses and the mule hidden there, and showed visible signs of impatience. His flat-featured face hardened into a grimace which augured ill for anyone who crossed him.

He withdrew, held a hasty council of war with his minions, and left the hiding pair in suspense for a little longer. He had not seen the significance of the narrow furrows running away from the door because Burke had lightly covered them with wisps of hay.

Presently the renegade leader thumped the front wall with the butt of his rifle.

'All right, Burke, I'm runnin' out of patience! I figured you were smarter than your brother! If you don't show yourself in the next minute I'm plannin' on settin' fire to this cabin of yours which took you so long to build! You hear me?'

Rusty Redman licked his dry lips and fingered his Winchester, while Burke, further over, applied a match to a carefully fashioned torch and prepared to put his offensive plan in motion. No less than three men were peering through the window now, Vic Redman having prudently withdrawn. It was clear to the occupants of the cabin that some sort of reception had been prepared for them.

Burke skilfully worked on the torch

until it flared at the tip. Before the smoke showed to the watchers in the cabin, he hurled the brand into the bale of hay in which the ends of the fuses were hidden.

The hay went up in a sudden roar. There were cries of surprise from the renegades who did not know how to react, or what, in fact, was happening to them. The burning bale held everyone's attention for about two minutes. Smoke swirled away from it, further disguising Burke's intentions, but eventually the watchers in the cabin spotted the sizzling fuses coming towards them. Even a person of low intelligence could read what was about to happen.

Suddenly, Vic Redman roared out an order. 'Arkensaw, get yourself through that door and stamp out that fuse! You hear me? *Pronto!* Hurry it up! Go, go go! Doggone it, there's another! Sundown, get out there an' back him up!'

While another man knocked glass out of the window on the near side, a preliminary to action with guns, the homely features of Arkensaw suddenly appeared. The stooping bow-legged figure leapt out, yelling either in terror or to give himself courage. He ran for a fuse which had about five yards to cover, but did not get there.

Two carefully aimed bullets from the rifle of Jabez Burke homed into his body. The first hit him in the chest, close to the breastbone. The second hit him in the back as he lost momentum and twisted in the air. He sank to the ground as the spluttering fuse ran along its special trench, passing him by.

A rifle fired through the window tried to pinpoint Burke without success. Sundown's stocky figure was framed in the door opening for a mere few seconds as the setback to Arkensaw registered. Mindful of his promise to assist, Rusty lined up on him and squeezed. The bullet had the effect of lifting the renegade's hat as he half-somersaulted backwards into the very temporary safety afforded by the cabin.

Rusty's second shot blasted more

glass out of the window.

'*Get down, Rusty!*'

The sudden warning came from the ex-soldier who knew to within a second or two when the explosion was due to take place. He also had a fair idea of the power which would be released in the charges which he had planted under the boards of his residence.

Rusty reacted quickly, throwing himself to the ground and closing his eyes. No reconnaissance for the period of the explosion. The ground in front of the shack appeared to heave and lurch to him, and then it shook and juddered and cascaded apart underneath the stout cabin.

Rusty counted three as the awful noise vibrations blasted his ear drums and the smell of dynamite and smoke assailed his nostrils. He glanced up cautiously and gaped as the logs which had formed the front wall were thrown up in the air like match sticks. Even the corpse of Arkensaw had been tossed aside by the blast. Of the other members of the gang, there were no signs. Creeping red and orange flames licked around what was left of the house shape.

Rusty found himself creeping across to where the destructive owner was regarding the holocaust with a satisfied saturnine expression on his face. Burke patted him on the shoulder as he came within touching distance, but kept his eyes focussed on the flaming ruin. Not so much as a silhouette had shown as the building went up. There was a strong chance that the other three had all died inside.

'Hell an' tarnation, Jabez, you certainly sorted that little outfit out! I suppose you'll reckon the Burkes are well revenged on the Redmans after this?'

'Eh? Oh, yes, I suppose so, young fellow. I shan't be leavin' for a while yet. I'll need to know if any of the rats survived. You, if you want, can ride back to where you left Laura. Tell her all's well, an' that I'll be along to join you as soon as I've seen to things.'

Rusty nodded and at the same time showed that he was puzzled.

'I've already thought of a place to take her, if that's what's bothering you,' Jabez shouted. 'We do have to be sure there are no survivors waitin' to take up the chase again, otherwise all this is for nothin'. You can see that, can't you?'

Rusty nodded and moved away. The burning building so held his attention that he stumbled several times before finding the spot where the grey stallion was tethered. He found himself wondering how Laura would make out with a man as ruthless as Jabez.

# 7

Progress was slow coming away from the scene of the action. Every few yards Rusty felt drawn to turn in the saddle and look back at the burning pyre which had started out as a simple westerner's log cabin. Burke kept well out of sight, and there were no signs at all of humans.

Presently, the dappled grey was far enough up the slope for intervening foliage to mask the fire, and the rider had perforce to turn his attention to the girl who awaited him. He found her crouching low in foliage not ten yards away from where he had left her. Her face was pale under the tan. Clearly, she was profoundly shocked by the shooting, the explosions and the demolition of the shack by fire.

'You, Rusty? You're all right? Where's Jabez? What happened? I didn't know what to think. He must have had a visit from my enemies, that's all I can think. Please, please tell me the worst!'

Rusty threw himself out of the saddle. Without thinking what he was doing he took her into his arms and patted the head which rested against his chest. In a few seconds, the girl became restless again, peering up into his grim face trying to read his thoughts.

'Jabez is all right. For a time, he didn't show himself. He had already observed a bunch of renegades approaching from the other direction. He guessed who they were and made preparations to get the better of them.'

'Who? Who were they, Rusty? I have to know!'

He gently released her and led her to a large boulder, where she seated herself. Fern fronds, growing high, swung backwards and forwards in a light breeze, fanning her gently as she waited nervously for news.

'He said they were Redman hirelings, and that proved to be true, I suppose, because before the shack went up a fellow callin' himself Vic Redman stepped into view and tried to bully him into showin' himself. This Redman threatened to burn down the shack if Jabez didn't come out and talk.'

'And eventually, I suppose, that's exactly what he did do,' Laura observed bitterly.

'Oh, no, it was Jabez who arranged to blow up the cabin. He had been expecting them and he placed dynamite charges underneath it, as soon as he knew they meant business. That is to say, they aimed to eliminate him as they did your husband. He set fire to long fuses and contrived to keep them in the building until it blew up.'

The girl was beating her knee with a small clenched fist. For several seconds she did not appear to have taken in Rusty's explanation of the explosion.

'He said to tell you not to worry about the cabin. He has already thought of an alternative place to take you.'

She nodded then. 'That's one thing about the Burkes. They're always reliable. I wish I could say as much for the Redmans. That — that villain callin' himself Vic Redman. It's scum such as he is that have made the name of Redman stink throughout the territory.'

Rusty removed his hat and scratched his head. He was puzzled. He propped himself up on the edge of the rock beside her.

'Laura, the way you talk, that fellow down there wasn't a Redman at all! How could you know he wasn't one of the clan?'

Her face hardened at the question. Her nostrils flared. She showed more spirit than he ever thought she had in her.

'I don't know that I ought to tell you, really, Rusty. But I will. You took me on trust, so here goes. The reason I know he's not a Redman is because *I* am a Redman myself! Old Man Redman was my father! There are no young male Redmans on the ranch now, or in

Redman City! That's how I know. You see now? I'm one of them! A direct descendant of the founder of the clan. So there.

'You might as well know also that I madc a break for it, slipped away from what was left of my family and did what I could to be rid of the hated name! I married Simeon Burke, a man who needed a wife. To some extent, it was a marriage of convenience. In one respect I married him for his name. In takin' his I turned my back on the name of Redman forever. Or so I thought.

'All I've succeeded in doin', though, is bringin' about my husband's death an' puttin' other men in danger. It's a sad, sordid story, I suppose. I've been round long enough to believe what many folks say, that the only good Redman is a dead one!'

After a short lapse of time, Laura became aware that her companion's reaction was not quite what she had expected.

'Well, aren't you goin' to say anythin'

now that you've heard it all?'

Rusty managed a grin, although it was not a very convincing one.

'My name is Redman, too. I was christened Russell Redman. When I broke my journey I was on my way to Redman City, goin' out of pure curiosity to visit with the Redmans, because my own close kin had left the country. It's only been in the last few hundred miles that I've begun to have doubts about the sort of people they are. I used to entertain hopes that they were distant cousins, or something like that, and that they would welcome me into their midst an' give me a chance to start a new life. Now, I'm not so sure.

'Things I've heard recently, and some of the happenings are makin' me feel my surname is not a good one to have. For the first time in my life I feel ashamed of it. Thinkin' back, Jeff More must have entertained doubts, but he didn't say anything about them. He jest gave me some advice about not gettin' involved, if I didn't like the way the city was run.'

Rusty suddenly found himself short of things to say. He turned his head away and toyed with his tobacco sack and a thin paper. He spilled the contents the first time and seemed surprised when Laura's hand came between his own and took away the makings.

She was smiling into his face and looking altogether desirable. There was a warmth in the intense green eyes which he had never seen before. He glanced down at the paper and the tobacco sack. Without moving either, he leaned across and lightly kissed her on the lips.

The sweet contact put more colour in her face. 'I'm sure you'll believe me, Rusty, when I say that life is full of surprises. All these miles we've ridden almost shoulder to shoulder an' neither of us knew that the other was a Redman. It's almost certain we ain't related, though. Whether that's a good thing or not, I don't know.'

Both of them were feeling a little bit embarrassed. The girl gave her full attention to the rolling of the cigarette and no further conversation took place until she had finished. She placed it between Rusty's lips and he brought a match stick out of his hat band with a delicate gesture. He struck it on his boot and applied it to the cigarette, drawing back so that the smoke would not go in Laura's face.

'Knowin' you are who you are has done something to me, Rusty. I don't know quite what it is, but it feels good. At the very least, you've made me believe once more that all Redmans are not evil. Maybe it means more than that to me, but that's all I've been able to figure out so far.

'Will you tell me something before life gets all involved again?'

Rusty rolled the cigarette around his mouth. He murmured: 'Anything. What do you most want to know?'

'I figure you must believe there's a lot

of truth in what folks in this territory say about the Redmans further west, that they're a bad lot an' so on. Will you still continue on your journey to visit them and see for yourself?'

Rusty frowned. He shrugged. 'What would you do in my place?'

'I can't answer that one, amigo. I'm a woman. I can't think like a man. You have to make up your own mind.'

The young man sank down into the grass. He allowed smoke to slowly trickle up above his head. Laura slid down beside him, patiently waiting for his answer.

'Well,' he began at last, 'I think I'll go a little closer. I could take Jeff More's advice an' not get involved, if everything is like it's supposed to be. On the other hand, I might jest find someone else in distress who wants a helpin' hand to get away. That way, I might stick around a little longer.'

Laura hid her face. She appeared to be examining her half boots with great curiosity. Clearly, she had not wanted

Rusty to go on to further hazards, west of the Pecos.

'Whatever happens, provided I don't find a bullet with my name on it, I'll be back to seek you out and renew our acquaintance. Maybe deepen it a little, if that's what you'd want.'

Laura gripped his arm and again laid her head on his shoulder.

'I can't say what's in my heart, Rusty. It has no right to be there, especially as I was married until quite recently. I'll have to go along with Jabez' protection for a while, now that he's committed himself in such a — a forthright fashion.'

Rusty nodded. The mention of Jabez again turned his mind back to the watch being kept at the shack. He thought, but did not speak his thoughts aloud, that Jabez was taking a long time over his watch. He stood up, having come to a decision.

'Now see here, Laura. I'm goin' back to make sure nothing's happened to him. You stick around for a few more minutes and then we'll all be out of this valley which has known so much violence.'

He pulled his Winchester out of the scabbard, gave the girl a hug, and set off down the slope on foot. In just a few minutes he crossed the open and ghosted into the first of the tree clumps on the low side of the grade.

Exercising the utmost caution, he flitted from tree to tree, gradually closing with the danger area. He was some seventy yards away when he saw Jabez clear the trees, mount up on his pinto and start towards him, leading the pack mule. Even at that distance, it was clear that Burke thought all danger over. He was relaxing in the saddle and letting the horse do all the work.

Rusty was about to stand clear and wave when he saw the other movement. It came from over to the left, on the lower ground not far from the creek bank. Vic Redman's roughly cut fair hair had been singed to the scalp. His face was blackened and bruised. His stetson was somewhere else. His shirt was a scorched rag around his shoulders and neck, but the rifle held in his two blackened hands looked as good as new.

Now, Rusty had a job to do. How to save Jabez from the man stalking him? The dark-haired young man knew intuitively that Redman would not be dissuaded from his purpose by coaxing, or even by harsh words. Only a bullet, or the immediate threat of death would put him off.

Before he could make up his mind exactly how to act, the survivor had the gun to his shoulder and was taking aim.

Rusty yelled: 'Redman! Over here!'

There was a pause of no more than a second or two, as the startled renegade reacted to the unexpected shout. By that time, Burke was alerted. He was flinging himself to the ground on the far side of his horse by the time the bullet whined towards him.

Vic Redman cursed in a querulous voice. Rusty put up his gun and the other peered around for him. One shot was all he was permitted before the other Redman sank into the long grass, but Rusty felt he might have winged him.

Burke fired a shot from where he had landed, and then started to slide along the ground, his movements not unlike those of a tail-less newt. There were only a few feet separating the pinto from the mule. He used the animals as a screen as he took his turn at the stalking.

For a time, no one appeared to make any progress. It was when Rusty shifted his ground and started to work his way nearer the creek that the uneven contest began to liven up. The true Redman was a little more noisy than he needed to be. His actions kept the enemy on the alert. Every now and then, Vic loosened off a bullet. On two occasions, his efforts were reasonably accurate. Rusty had his shirt singed at the waist. Another bullet narrowly missed his white bandanna.

The trees were fast thinning out on the dry, gentle slope down to the water when Vic came suddenly to his feet, momentarily saw Rusty in his sights, and prepared to dispose of him.

Burke, having made a lot of ground with his movements masked by the animals, saw him at the critical moment. A sixth sense, or perhaps just nerves, made Rusty dive down the slope as the guns crashed.

Vic's bullet went over his head. Burke's shell ripped into Vic's rib cage from the side and dropped him sprawling down the slope, his heart already giving out.

For nearly a minute, Burke stayed where he was, out of sight. Rusty crawled forward another few feet and stuck his tired head into the cool waters. The other Redman was dead. Five minutes later, Burke stood beside Rusty, who was still slopping water over himself.

'Laura all right?'

'Sure. She's waitin' for us.'

'It's a darned good thing you came lookin' for me. I'd jest convinced myself that this carrion, Vic, had died in the shack with the others not accounted for. He would have had me if you hadn't distracted him. I'm obliged to you.'

Rusty nodded and stood up. 'I'm glad it's all over, Jabez. What are we goin' to do now? We can't bring Laura down to the scene of all this carnage.'

'Nice thinkin', Rusty. Especially, as we don't figure to give out any Christian burials.'

'We jest keep on ridin' out then. Is that it?'

'You could collect the spare ridin' horses if you want something to do. I'm thinkin' of takin' Laura to a relay station further south a piece. A few extra horses would reimburse the girl an' me for our losses in regard to the Redmans. Yer, I like that idea. Bring them along with you, Rusty. We'll camp up there, where Laura's waitin', an' then we'll clear out. If there's any more trouble in store for us, it'll have to come lookin'.'

'All right, I'll collect the horses, Jabez, an' then I'll be right along. Don't say too much about the in-fightin' down here. Laura's nerves are bad, an we don't want her to have nightmares.'

Burke acknowledged with a sober nod of his head. He backtracked, mounted up and left Rusty to his chore.

# 8

Three days later, Rusty was some thirty miles on the other side of the Pecos river. He had crossed the impressive waterway on a poled raft ferry the day after he left Laura and Jabez to make their way to the relay station. Even now, he was not altogether sure that he had made the right decision. Nightly, he felt himself yearning for the pretty young widow with the special problems appertaining to her kin and name.

Laura, he felt sure, was as much drawn to him as he was to her, and yet she could not plainly make her feelings known on account of her too-recent bereavement. Jabez had studied the bond between them, and he had refrained from saying too much. Burke's mind on the question of Rusty being a Redman had remained closed. He had not offered any sort of hostility, and yet a certain coolness had arrived with the new knowledge.

As the grey stallion jogged away beneath him over open ground, Rusty decided that he was probably a fool. Laura was the smart Redman. She had made it away, albeit at some cost: but she was still free and with every passing day her prospects were surely improving. One Redman away, and another placidly heading into known trouble.

He turned in the saddle and fished in his saddle-bag, producing from it a big neck square; a bandanna which was different from any other he had seen. It was, in fact, two squares of cloth sewn one on top of the other. One side of it was all red, and the other was all black. He frowned as he tried to recall the exact words Laura had used when she gave it to him.

'Rusty, take this,' she had advised. 'Don't make a point of showin' it to everyone you see. In fact, I'd keep it out of sight most of the time. There's jest a chance you might get in a tight spot with Redman hirelings sometime, and then it might help you. Maybe they wouldn't shoot straight away, if you showed it.'

He squeezed it in his hand, and then released it again. It sprang back into shape. As he pondered morosely about this and that, a faint perfume came up from it, a scent which he would always associate with Laura. A talisman of sorts, with Laura's perfume on it. He wondered if he would ever feel the need to use it.

Half an hour later, at two o'clock on a hot afternoon, he jumped the dappled grey across a narrow creek and, incidentally, into trouble.

Nothing happened at first. He walked the stallion up a hill slope, through straggling patches of scrub and occasional tree stands. He ought to have been warned when he saw a small group of longhorns off to his left, but he was riding in the most trying part of the day and it did not occur to him that he was riding on private range, and that it might provoke trouble.

A gap-toothed cowpuncher with a permanent sun squint and a broken-brimmed stetson stuck his head out of a hollow on the right, and stared unbelievingly as Rusty went by. The waddy in question, who had been calmly passing the timc of day in the nicest possible way he knew, promptly whistled for his partner who was asleep behind him and also out of sight.

Rusty heard the whistle and turned in the saddle. The first man rose fully into view and pointed at him.

'Hey, mister, you're on Diamond E property! Did you know that?'

Flashing his most winning smile, Rusty shook his head. 'Nope, I didn't. Bein' a stranger in these parts, I wouldn't have known anyways, unless I'd tripped over a cow with a Diamond E markin' on it. I'm obliged to you, in any case. Adios, amigo.'

Rusty raised his hand in salute and urged the grey forward again. He could tell by the expression on the cowpuncher's face that he was not satisfied for a stranger to ride on across the territory of his master, but sometimes a bluff paid off. This seemed to be a likely time to try it.

'*Hold it right there!*'

The second utterance addressed to the intruder sounded much more formidable. For a few seconds, he did not know exactly where the challenge had come from. Consequently, as he did not want to prompt any hostile bullets, he reined in and sat back.

The man who had challenged him a second time was off to the right again. He had scrambled out of the far side of the hollow in which the first man had been resting. Instead of a bewildered expression, he had with him a business-like rifle to back up his demands. It was pointed directly at Rusty's trunk.

'Are you an ordinary hold-up man, or do you treat all visitors in this slightly hostile fashion?'

'Raise your hands!'

The man with the gun was a short, hefty barrel-chested individual in his early forties. He had the pronounced red face of a perpetual beer drinker, and he carried over twenty pounds in excess body weight. When Rusty had answered him, his round blood-shot eyes had looked slightly taken aback. In spite of the steadiness of the pointing gun, his eyes behind it suggested that he was not at all sure if his order would be complied with. Rusty shrewdly noted this and acted upon it.

'Mister, I assume you're a little impatient, havin' had your afternoon sleep interrupted, but I don't want to raise my hands. I'm tired, too. If there's anything else you have to say to me, get it off your chest an' then I'll be goin'. I have a long way to travel.'

The gunman's thick lips opened and shut. If his partner had not approached Rusty on foot with a revolver in his hand, he would have undoubtedly backed off and tried to save his face.

Gap-tooth's intervention prevented this.

'Mr Madigan, the foreman, told us that on no account was we ever to let strangers cross this territory. Now, you're a stranger, an' *I* think the best thing you can do is come back with us to the home buildings an' explain yourself. That is, unless you want to do things Pallin's way. He's the one with the rifle. Not exactly predictable, if you know what I mean.'

Rusty thought over the situation for a few seconds. After the practice he had had in recent times, he felt he could have thrown himself out of the saddle and given a good account of himself against these two determined waddies. The heat of the day and the desire for a smooth passage prevented him from forcing a showdown.

'Tell your friend to put down his gun, an' I'll ride over to talk with Mr Madigan. How will that be? Only, no hand raisin' an' no foolin' about.'

Pallin said: 'Dickie Akers, you

shouldn't have interfered!'

But already, the stouter of the two was putting up his gun and going off in search of his riding horse. The one referred to as Dickie Akers kept his revolver in full view, but he grinned more or less easily and tried to give Rusty the impression that the heat was off.

Two minutes later, the trio were headed in a northerly direction. Pallin led, his shortness of leg seemingly emphasized as he sat the saddle of his buckskin. Rusty followed him up, about ten yards behind, making no effort to push his grey to any extent. Dickie Akers brought up the rear on a long-legged claybank with an uneven way of trotting. Akers whistled a popular tune normally played to the guitar. He was off the note most of the time. His musical effort constituted all the action on the way in.

The home buildings of the cattle ranch seemed closely crowded together, and singularly lacking in paint. Hens scuttled about all over the place instead of being penned in. It had the air of being other than a paying concern.

The two escorts made a bit of noise as they entered the open area in front of the house. A Mexican cook briefly showed himself from the cookhouse beyond the bunkhouse. An elderly blacksmith with a permanent stoop came to see what the excitement was, and then retired to his quiet work room.

On the gallery of the house was the owner. Lon Elders was over sixty years of age. The last few years he had been heaving himself around on a crutch, due to a damaged hip; pain made him look his age. His eyes had a washed-out look. He was tall, thin and spare in a shirt and denims faded and washed to near-whiteness. A straw hat hid his bald crown. Elders banged with his crutch on the top rail of the gallery as the three riders lined up by the hitch rail in front of the house with Rusty in the middle. He could see it was trouble of some sort, but he did not feel like dealing with it.

Two people came out from the house, both females. Conchita Elders was nearly ten years younger than her husband. She was half Mexican and half white American. The rigorous life she had led as a rancher's wife had filled out her figure to vast proportions. Thick, greying dark hair stood out from her head like wire.

Mariella, the daughter of the marriage, was — if anything — darker skinned than her mother. She looked older than her sixteen years. Her hair was long, and a medium shade of brown. Her figure, dressed habitually in an off-white blouse and a dark skirt, had long since filled out. She crossed the gallery with a tea cloth in her hand. Her broad flat feet made no sound in open sandals.

The son of the marriage, Alvar, was whiter-skinned, a freckled beanpole of a boy in cut-down denims. He came from the direction of the smithy.

The rancher looked edgy. He peered fiercely in all directions as if he expected his overworked foreman to materialize out of the air, took a swig of moonshine from a glass on the table beside him, and cleared his throat.

'Well, well? What have you two waddies been up to *this* time?'

Pallin, the stout waddy, dismounted and respectfully touched his hat. 'Mr Elders, Madigan said no strangers were allowed to cross your land. This character happened along where we were workin'. He couldn't give a proper account of himself, so we brought him along to make his explanations at the house.'

'Oh, all right. You did the proper thing, I suppose, but Madigan will have to talk to him. See where he is, will you? He's around here some place.'

Somewhere round the back of the house a man coughed heavily as though he had phlegm on his chest. At once, the old man relaxed and his wife and daughter retired into the house. Rusty,

124

who was tired of sitting and being inspected, dismounted. Dickie Akers did the same and dashed off to intercept the foreman.

Madigan was a thick-set forty-five year old with a red chin beard, a bald head and protruding blue eyes. He was bare-headed. His checkered shirt was open down the front revealing a very hirsute chest. He walked right up to Rusty, making nothing of the fact that he was some two to three inches shorter.

'How come you was found wanderin' about on Diamond E territory, stranger?'

Rusty, determined not to be annoyed until he felt like it, grinned, nodded and remarked: 'I was travellin' west. I didn't see any boundary line. I admit my error. On thinkin' back, I suppose your boundary was the creek I crossed earlier.'

Madigan backed off a foot or so, and flexed his arm muscles.

'It ain't much of an explanation, is it?

125

Are you sure you weren't sent here by the Box W outfit to cause trouble? Goodness knows they've got enough hired men with guns these days. I put it to you, you could be here spyin'. Now, what do you say to that?'

'I say I've never heard of the Box W before. I've never been west of the Pecos before this week. I believe something's riled you today an' that you're determined to make trouble where there is none.'

Madigan coloured up. The redness started at his neck and worked its way into his face. His eyes seemed even more prominent than usual.

'Now look you here, amigo, nobody — nobody talks to me that way on a spread where I'm the ramrod. I've a good mind to teach you a lesson.'

The foreman shifted his stance so that he looked like a prize-fighter. Rusty had a feeling that he had been one at some period in his life. The latter patted his chest and wondered if this was the time to show a bit of temper, or to play it cool.

Madigan sidled closer, until he could have scored with a short-arm jab. He clenched his right fist, waved it about a bit, glanced sideways to see how the old man on the gallery was taking it, and then received a sharp jab on the chin from Rusty.

The dark-haired young man had just seen in a flash the faces of Vic Redman, Richy Malone, Skinner Grouch and a few other unsavoury characters he had come up against. Madigan, caught off balance, narrowly missed the hind legs of Akers' claybank and landed on his hands and knees, absolutely fuming.

Rusty turned his back on him, pushed Pallin out of his way, and swung back into leather. Madigan started to rise and come for him at the run, but a big shotgun suddenly pointing from the gallery slowed everything down.

'Get down offen that hoss, an' raise your hands, real slow!'

Madigan held back, hesitating. This was one of the few times when he had seen the owner make a positive move. Rusty also hesitated. If he dived for the ground, his mount would get the full force of the shotgun's load, and he did not want that to happen. So he complied.

As soon as he was on the ground with his hands half raised, the two attendant waddies lifted his .45 Colt and the Winchester which was in the saddle scabbard.

'My name, if you want to put it in your visitors' book, is Redman. Russell Redman.'

Madigan, who had planned to strike him while his hands were raised, checked himself again. The old man gasped. So did the small boy who was observing from the other side of the yard. Pallin dumped the revolver on the gallery as though it had suddenly become red hot. Akers reverently laid the Winchester near it.

'Lock him up! In the empty stable,' the old man ordered, when he had recovered from the shock. 'You hear me, you two good for nothin' waddies, get a move on! Every time you make a move there's trouble for the spread. I don't know why Madigan employs you!'

'Oh, yes, you do, Mr Elders. It's because the right sort of workers don't want to come here.'

The foreman's tone implied low wages and bad working conditions. Rusty gave the owner the most savage glare he could conjure up before he went off round the side of the building with one waddy armed and watching him on either side.

The stable had one high window, too small to climb through. It was dry and not particularly uncomfortable. A person not specially keen on the smell of horses would have suffered, but Rusty was not in that category. He settled down, in a corner, as soon as he knew the padlock on the outside of the door was strong enough to hold him in. He took off his hat and his boots, fiddled with his tobacco sack and his matches, and wondered why he had not been bright enough to invent a cock-and-bull story about a large group of Redman hirelings looking for him across Diamond E range. Friendly Redmans, of course. With the match in his hand, he wondered if he could do himself any harm by firing the straw, but mindful of the violent end of other Redman hirelings, he merely lit his cigarette and smoked.

\* \* \*

Around one in the morning he was aroused by a whisper at the window. Earlier, the girl had handed in food and coffee without conversing. Now, after everyone else had retired, she was back with her small brother and a proposition.

'Mr Redman, your presence frightens us all. Perhaps Mr Madigan was wrong to treat you the way he did. If we — my brother and I — release you, will you go straight back to your friends? I mean clear off this ranch and not go to our rivals in the range war at the Box W?'

'Mr Madigan was wrong, miss, an' I accept your offer. Provided I can have my horse, my weapons and that I can ride on in the direction I was headin' when the waddies took over.'

He muscled up to the window and looked out to assure himself that this was not a Madigan trick to get at him in the night. There were no signs of treachery. The girl undid the lock while the small boy, Alvar, went off to saddle the grey and bring it around.

In one of the buildings a dog barked, but no one took any notice. Alvar came back leading the grey and also his own pony. Mariella, the girl, thanked him for agreeing to their plan, and Rusty in his turn thanked them for assisting his withdrawal. Alvar, feeling his importance in this clandestine arrangement, then took the lead and speedily led Rusty to the spot where he had first been challenged.

'Jest keep ridin' to the west, Mr

Redman, till you clear our range. Adios. I hope we never see you again.'

'Those are my sentiments, young fellow. I hope you don't get into trouble for settin' me free.'

They parted quickly. Fortunately, the grey seemed as keen as its master to get beyond Diamond E soil.

# 9

Two days of steady saddle travel brought Rusty to the outskirts of Freedom Falls, county town of the area which encompassed Redman City, at ten o'clock in the morning. From a distance he could see that the town was well laid out. It had a square and a court house, a church and two or three blocks of offices in the centre and three or four parallel streets on either side of the central thoroughfare.

On the last furlong he had been musing further about the name of Redman. In this territory, it always provoked a response of one sort or another. No one was unimpressed by it. Names like Smith or Garcia meant little on the average man's tongue, but Redman, that was different. The name always made others stop and think. Most folks were apprehensive of it. On

Diamond E land, some thirty miles back, it had so scared the owner's family that they had released him rather than incur further trouble from the notorious clan.

This town, Freedom Falls, was reputed to be free of Redman influence. It had its own administration, not interfered with or swayed by the Redman faction entrenched on territory to the south-west. And yet it had an atmosphere. The folks who walked the streets all looked thoughtful and mildly apprehensive of one another. Rusty wondered if they had some special local problem, or whether the apparent tension had anything to do with Redman influence.

He decided to find out gradually. His first call was at a livery stable on the west side of town. He had been directed to the biggest in the settlement and when he arrived there, he realised that the owner was in the freight business as well as that of stabling horses.

The big sliding door of the stable was

open, showing a double line of stalls. There were two vacant ones, one on either side. As soon as Rusty's eyes were accustomed to the indoor gloom, he glanced around him, looking for an ostler to take the grey. No one appeared to be on duty. The loft, a favourite relaxing spot for tired or lazy stable hands, was empty.

Down the side of the building was a passage wide enough to take a wagon. In the rear wall were two doors, one of which was ajar. Voices carried faintly into the building from the area at the rear where a used farm cart was drawn up.

The newcomer wondered about shouting for service, but he thought better of it, and himself ran the grey into a stall and started to strip it. While he was busy, the breeze blew open the rear door so that the voices carried more clearly.

Having entered the town full of curiosity, Rusty found it more than passing easy to eavesdrop. He had the impression that two or three farmers were negotiating to buy the cart from the freight and livery boss.

'All right, all right, so the price you're offerin' is a fair one,' the boss acknowledged. 'I can't say fairer than that. That isn't my problem. I have freighters on the trails around here all the time. But I have to be wary of the Redmans. If ever they learned I'd been sellin' to you boys from the ghost town they'd hit my wagons between towns.

'I can't afford to run an armed guard every trip. As sure as fate my freightin' business would be gradually ruined. You can see how it is. I'll allow you've suffered yourselves. But you'll see my side of the problem.'

A cautious head peered in through the open door to make sure that they were not overheard. Somehow, Rusty anticipated the move. He contrived to be bending down in the stall at the time when he should have been observed.

The conversation was resumed.

Another voice said: 'If we don't get

this cart we'll never stand a chance of gettin' on our feet, Mr Jones. It's more than a day's drive to the ghost town, an' we know you don't want us to be seen leavin' here with the cart. So, we have a plan.

'We'll wait until sundown, and then slip out of town. About a mile down the track there's an old barn. It lacks a roof. We can stay there until near sun-up and then move on. What do you say?'

There must have been about two minutes of doubt and head shaking, but eventually the freighter agreed. Rusty started to whistle then while he worked. He finished grooming the grey and showed surprise when the liveryman came in from the back.

The buyers slipped away by the side alley, and Rusty worked hard to give the impression that he had heard nothing of the secret transaction. Ostler Jones, a tall thin man in a grey shirt, scuffed boots and baggy trousers accepted him at his face value and fetched a bag of oats for the stallion.

Towards noon, Rusty booked a room, swilled himself down under a pump, shaved and changed, and eventually settled before a hearty lunch. He slept for an hour on his hotel bed and then wandered out to seek beer and information. Quite by chance, he came across a man he took to be one of those in the cart buying deal. He asked permission to sit at the same table in the saloon, and courteously provided the farmer with a glass of beer. Clint Noakes, the farmer in question, was lean and muscular. He looked older than his thirty-six years. He had red hair, a lantern jaw and was dressed in bibbed overalls and a fawn stetson.

'Thanks for the beer, stranger, it always tastes better when another man pays for it. Something I can do for you?'

Rusty grinned and nodded. 'I'm movin' west, lookin' for a place to settle. I heard tell there was a ghost town of some sort about due west.

Maybe you've heard of it. Would there be any sort of opportunity for a hard workin' fellow to settle there an' make himself a few bucks?'

Noakes' face hardened. He stared hard at Rusty as though the question was a deliberate leg pull. He was slow in answering.

'There has to be a reason why a thrivin' town becomes a ghost town. How did this one lose its life?' Rusty prompted.

Noakes studied all the tables near at hand. He was a long time before he decided that they were out of ear-shot of anyone. Even then, he was reluctant to give his views.

'Big Bend became a ghost town because a few years back its population didn't take kindly to domination from Redman City. The Redmans went to work on it, took away its life blood, one way and another. Now, it's a place where outcasts from Redman City live, an' folks who are too stubborn to move away.

'My advice is worth more than half a dozen beers. Stay away, young fellow. Don't get involved. You hear me? Don't give the Redmans any notion to interfere with you.'

Almost at once, a thoughtful-looking deputy and one or two local drinkers started to filter through the tables. Their approach had the effect of terminating Noakes' advice. The farmer suddenly became restless. He came to his feet in something of a hurry, murmured his thanks again for the beer and made his way into the street without a backward glance. Rusty drank two more beers and slowly smoked a cigarette before he left the saloon. In that time, he had come to a decision. He would visit the ghost town next, before going on to Redman City.

★ ★ ★

Between nine p.m. and midnight, Freedom Falls achieved a certain amount of hilarity unbeknown during the hours of daylight. With the lighting of the lamps the townsfolk seemed to see fewer disturbing shadows over their shoulders. The honky-tonk pianos, the free-flowing beer and the music and dancing in the larger establishments seemed to banish a lot of their undeclared fears.

Nevertheless, Rusty Redman retired to his room early with his head full of disturbing notions about places west. He was tired, and yet he could not sleep. He had visions of the farmers slipping along to the livery like Indians and spiriting away the farm cart which they so greatly needed.

Freedom Falls *was* suffering because of Redman influence. It was a reasonably run town, and yet its citizens acted as if they were living in the shadow of evil; as if some great calamity could come their way at any time, unwanted and unbidden.

Suddenly, Rusty was out of his bed and pacing around in his bare feet. As the bell in the clock tower tolled the hour of midnight, he knew beyond a shadow of a doubt what he ought to be doing. He ought to be offering his services to the farmers and riding along with them to the ghost town. He thought about the prospect from all angles. For a man determined to explore further, this was a fine way to do it.

He dressed hurriedly, pulled on his boots and gathered together his gear. No one was manning the counter in the foyer. He wrote a note to say that he was urgently called away, left sufficient money to cover one night's lodgings, and moved out into the street.

There would be somebody at the livery, on account of the cart being spirited away: or so he thought. But the stable, when he arrived, was deserted. Rather than disturb the resting horses with a lot of prowling and calling, he walked the grey out with the minimum of noise and saw to the saddling in the passage.

He left the ostler's dues on the dusty

desk in the tiny office. The cart had gone from its earlier resting place. That pleased him. He mounted up in front of the building, allowed the grey to turn on the spot and himself took account of the fading man-made noises down the street.

A piano accompanied a few drinkers' raucous voices. In another building there was a lot of noise, caused mostly by the banging of beer mugs and voices raised in argument. Gradually, the county seat was losing its nightly vitality.

Rusty straightened his back, braced his shoulders and pointed the reluctant stallion towards the west. The moon was full and powerful. The rider wondered what it augured for the immediate future, if anything.

His night vision was reasonably good. On this particular trail, although the traffic had fallen off, the going was fairly easy and the track clearly marked. The grey stepped along it with assurance in its gait, in spite of the shadows thrown faintly towards it from encroaching rocks, scrub and an occasional stunted tree.

Here and there, the metal-rimmed wheels of the cart had left sign. Rusty noted it and mused on the distance. To some westerners three hundred yards was sometimes talked of as a mile. To others, an ordinary mile was nearer two.

The conjecture on this occasion was short-lived. Not far short of a true mile, the rider caught sight of a flickering light off on the right, to the north of the trail. He recollected that the man at the livery had said the barn had no roof, and he guessed correctly that the light carried from inside the building.

So as not to upset the men who did not want to be observed, he kept all noise to a minimum. Intuition warned him that all was not well when he still had a couple of hundred yards to go. He dismounted, cupped the muzzle of the grey, warning it to be silent, and continued his approach.

The barn was of wood. Its walls were filled in, except for a wide opening in the long side facing the track. The flickering had to come from a torch, or torches. The light did not suggest a lamp. He slipped his Winchester clear of the scabbard, urged the grey on to a patch of grass and went forward on foot.

There were several men inside the building and horses, too. There was coarse laughter, and some sort of contest or struggle taking place. In front of the building was a horse trough and a bucket. Rusty noted these as he ghosted forward. At the rear were other horses, fully saddled up and ready for the trail. The farmers were having one of the confrontations they dreaded.

Oddly enough, no one paid any attention to the out of doors. He went close enough to know that there were two torches burning inside and that one of the farmers was receiving a beating from two or three other men.

Not knowing how spirited the farmers were, he did not know quite how to spring his surprise. Meanwhile, the cart horses snickered in panic. The punch-up experts were goaded on, and occasionally someone offered a sharp word of protest.

Rusty put down his Winchester and instead took up the water bucket. He filled it without taking his eyes off the opening and advanced on his boot toes until he could see inside. The cart and the horses were in the background. Closer, the red-headed farmer, with whom he had taken beer, was systematically being beaten up between three hard-faced trail-riding gunmen.

Blood trickled from Noakes' face. He parried blows where he could, but his stamina was almost sapped. One of his assailants was a fair-bearded slugger with a lot of muscle and a promising paunch. Another was a lean Mexican with a bandit moustache and curved sideburns. His curly brown hair glistened with perspiration. His steeple hat jerked at the nape of his neck as he moved. The third man was younger: deadpan blue killer's eyes belied the fact that he was not long past twenty-one years of age. His stetson had a turned-up brim. He fought with his mouth open. Perspiration showed under the arms of his fringed buckskin tunic.

On either side of the doorway looking inwards were two others. One was a shifty-looking character in a brown suit with high cheekbones and narrowed eyes. His stetson was also brown in colour, and under his jacket he had a white shirt and a string tie. He held his torch steady and clenched his teeth as he watched the slaughter.

The fifth man was in his late teens, a trigger-happy baby-faced killer with fair down-like stubble on his chin and upper lip. He favoured a completely black outfit. In his excitement, he had to hold his torch with both hands to stop it waving about and putting up a smoke screen.

Two farmers were holding on to four shaft horses, while the third had his back to a cart wheel, which he gripped frenziedly, having nothing better to do. These three were the first to notice the late-comer. Their mouths were wide-open but unobserved, as Rusty hurled his bucket of water over the torch held by the baby-faced youth.

The torch went out at once, and the youth staggered back, half-drenched, and thoroughly startled. The man in the brown suit ground out an oath, shifted the torch to his right hand and prepared to retaliate, while the three bullies in the centre suddenly hauled off with their fists clenched and raised.

Rusty's senses were very much on the alert. He had the insight to know that he was about to face one of the major crises of his brief, but exciting career.

# 10

Mindful that he was likely to face five sets of hostile guns in a matter of seconds, Rusty danced clear of the entrance again. Crouching by the trough, he awaited the attack. The youngster in black came first. He was discomfited when the thrown bucket hit his head and caused him to stumble.

Next came the man in the brown suit, still carrying his torch in one hand and hefting a revolver in the other. Rusty aimed steadily and shot him through the chest. He went down and stayed that way, his torch rolling away from him towards the trough. Indoors, there were sounds of fistic exchanges as the farmers retaliated in desperation. One man had picked up a piece of timber and was laying about him with it.

Noakes, lacking power in his arms,

kicked one of his adversaries hard in a vital spot. Still watching the entrance, Rusty picked up the fallen torch. As he did so, the stunned youth in black scuttled away on his hands and knees.

In an instant, the burning brand sailed over the wall and dropped amid the struggling men. It had been intended to further distract the attackers and it did just that. A farmer grabbed it and used it to fend off an assailant.

At the critical stage, the Redman hirelings panicked.

The bearded heavyweight, the Mexican and the blue-eyed killer in the buckskin outfit all made for the door at once. A thoroughly ruthless gunman could have cut them all down, silhouetted as they were with the flickering torch light at their backs.

The heavyweight had two guns drawn. In his anxiety to pinpoint the enemy, he tripped over the bucket and Rusty was enabled to get close and hit him over the head with his revolver barrel. The Mexican side-stepped the fallen figure and the dead one. He had a revolver in his left hand and a knife in the other. A hefty blow across the forearm made him part with his gun, and a timely kick on the side of the neck made him drop the knife. He wriggled away, painfully, on his knees.

No sooner had the Mexican's silhouette separated from that of Rusty than the remaining gunman raised both his weapons and started to fire from the hip. One bullet narrowly missed Rusty's waist. Another missed his right cheek. Rusty gritted his teeth and fired back, aiming for the body. Two bullets had homed into the buckskin tunic before its wearer slowly sank down and stopped firing.

A fourth bullet helped the heavy-weight on his way, cutting a groove in the ground between his feet as he staggered upright and turned away. The remaining bullets in the gun helped speed the Mexican round the corner. By that time, Rusty was standing with his feet apart, absolutely breathless due to the speed of the action.

He groped for the brown-suited man's gun, knowing his own was empty. At the rear, there were sounds of men mounting up in a hurry. Noakes came out next, also gasping for breath, but dying to get in a telling shot. Side by side, Rusty and the farmer blasted at the three withdrawing riders. This time, however, the moving targets proved elusive.

Another farmer came out, and surveyed the exterior of the barn. In answer to a call from inside, he filled his lungs: 'It's all over, Windy, we've survived! Tell Phil not to worry any more!'

Dried out and jaded, the four farmers and Rusty went indoors and belated introductions took place. Phil Savage, the deaf one, was a stooping grey-bearded man in a derby hat. He looked his sixty years. Windy Neumann was in his late forties, a bulky red-faced sod-buster with thinning fair hair hidden under an undented hat. Jay Paris was fifty-odd. He had a short black moustache, beetle brows and a steeple straw hat.

Clint Noakes, the lantern-jawed redhead encountered in the saloon, did most of the early talking.

Rusty explained: 'I heard a whole lot of talk when you were at the back of the livery tryin' to buy the cart. I thought then you were the sort of folks I'd like to help. You told Jones how you planned to come to this barn and hang on until daylight. I was lying restless on my bed, and suddenly I couldn't keep away.'

There was a chorus of sincere thanks, but the farmers soon dried up on that score and began to think of the future.

'What do we do now?' Paris asked heavily, surveying his crushed steeple hat. 'They'll be bound to come out at us again before we get home.'

Neumann and the elderly Savage were in poor spirits. Only Noakes, battered and bruised over his rib cage, and abdomen, seemed to have any fight left in him. 'I put it to you, friends, we've worked hard to get this cart. We ought to try an' keep it. We can't jest give in meekly because we fear reprisals, can we?'

'You think they'll attack you again?' Rusty queried.

'Certain sure, they will,' Paris returned bluntly. 'Our only chance is to push on without waitin' for sunrise. As like as not, those three survivors will try to get the better of us before we make the ghost town. Otherwise, they'll lose face with the boys who sent them over to fix us.'

'I aim to visit the ghost town, so count me in on this,' Rusty suggested. 'How would it be if you set off real soon, an' I came along behind, as a rear guard?'

Rusty thumbed bullets into his Colt while they thought about it.

'I don't think they'll come at us from the front,' Noakes observed. 'Maybe it's a good idea at that. If you don't mind gettin' yourself further involved.'

Paris agreed. He also pushed Neumann and Savage to approve, as well. Rusty put the two spare riding horses into the barn as soon as the shaft horses and the vehicle were clear. He shook hands briefly with the farmers, and turned his attention to the dead men.

★　★　★

The cart had a start of fifteen minutes. Rusty then followed up slowly, keeping some two hundred yards to the rear. Some two hours later, when the self-appointed rear guard was feeling very sleepy, the terrain changed. On either side of the trail, which had narrowed, rock formations bulked and overhung the track.

He studied a pair of stunted oak trees, one growing close on either hand. His trail weariness suggested a trap of some sort, which would operate while he slept. He rigged a lariat across the gap from one tree to the other, about eighteen inches above the ground.

He had been curled up behind a rock for no more than twenty minutes when the horse-riding trio started to approach. No one spoke as they advanced towards the critical spot. In a bunch, they hit the rawhide, all the horses being deceived by it. Amid muted cries of alarm, the three gun slingers were precipitated earthwards. Babyface in the black outfit crashed heavily on his neck and shoulders, and stayed down. The bearded heavyweight struck his head on a trail-side rock and was rendered unconscious. The Mexican came out of it best, although one of his ankles suffered.

Rusty stepped out in front of the horses. Only one had sufficient courage after the fall to try and make a get-away. He grabbed its reins and managed to stop it in a few yards. A warning bullet between the boots stopped the Mexican from trying to retaliate. He was disarmed and made to hold the horses while the other two, slowly recovering, were checked for arms and made to mount up.

The dark-haired young man was determined to take them back to the town jail. He was annoyed with himself because he would have to backtrack some distance, but he figured it had to be done. If the authorities in the county were to be alerted to operate against the Redmans, this was as good a way to prompt them as any.

No one tried to make a break for it as they back-tracked to the old barn, all the time menaced by Rusty's Winchester from the rear. Lopez, the Mexican, remarked that the Redmans would hunt down the interfering stranger and hang him, but all he got for his pains was a clout over the head with a six-gun barrel.

'You, Mex, dismount. Go into that barn. You'll find two bodies there, an' two horses. Load the two corpses on to the back of the white stallion, an' bring the claybank here to me.'

The swarthy man, who had had

experience of loading dead bodies on to reluctant horses before, protested. Rusty clicked the hammer of his Colt. That had the effect of speeding the action. When five minutes had gone by, the controlling rider betrayed impatience.

'If you aren't out soon, I'm comin' in there to shoot you. I feel like goin' on without you!'

'Pronto, pronto, senor! Give me time!'

Lopez' manners suddenly improved. He came out limping almost at once, leading the two horses. The heavyweight, who answered reluctantly to the name of Brent, took over the reins of the doubly-laden stallion. Notchy, the baby-faced killer, had nothing at all to say while stripped of his guns.

With half an hour to go before sunrise, the tired riding group re-entered the county town and plodded up the main street as far as the sheriff's office. There was a lamp burning, but no one around. Frowning with weariness, Rusty made the best of it.

Notchy and Lopez brought in the dead and laid them out on the floor. Brent was the first to submit to having his hands tied behind him. He went into the cell in the rear wall. Young Notchy followed him, Lopez went in last. Rusty locked the door and came away, making use of the lamp over the desk to leave a message.

He wrote: *To the county sheriff.*

*These five men, two dead and three who ought to be, assaulted with intent to rob and kill four farmers from Big Bend. The assault occurred at the old barn one mile out of town towards the ghost town. It is suggested that these scum should be held in jail for as long as possible. The intended victims can be interviewed at Big Bend any time. In the near future, respectable citizens of the ghost town and Redman City will need help in restoring decent law and* order. Any self-respecting county sheriff will not decline to assist.

Yours sincerely,

A lover of law and order.

Leaving the note in a prominent place on the sheriff's desk, Rusty doffed his hat to the three angry renegades and quietly closed the door after him. The sky in the east was turning from black to grey as he rode out of town once more, forking the dappled grey and leading the claybank as spare.

★ ★ ★

The hundred or so folks who lived in the ghost town still liked to believe that it looked depopulated to a casual wayfarer. Its inhabitants had been gradually filtering in for upwards of three years. The more folks who lived there, the more difficult it was to make prowling Redman hirelings believe that they did not amount to much.

Originally, the town of Big Bend had run to between two and three hundred buildings, ranged mostly in lines along six streets. Anyone prowling about and looking for trouble usually gave their attention to the buildings on the periphery or along the central thoroughfare which had once been known as Lincoln Avenue.

Bearing this in mind, the dour displaced citizens who still contrived to thrive in the ghost town mostly had their homes in the in-between streets. In other words, the outer buildings were left entirely alone to get on with their decaying. Likewise the saloons, offices, stores and hotels which had once graced the Avenue.

The quartet of farmers reached Big Bend some three hours after sunrise. In ordinary circumstances, they would have chatted with their families, taken a meal and then gone off to bed to catch up on their sleep. On this particular occasion, however, such a course of action was scarcely possible.

In the first place, Noakes and his comrades still had sufficient energy to want to recount their fortunate brush with the Redman renegades. That, in itself, took quite a time to talk about. Prominent among those who had revelled in the details were Sandy Paris, the son of Jay Paris, who had been to Freedom Falls, and Richy Noakes, the younger brother of Clint Noakes, the first of the four farmers to make Rusty's acquaintance.

Having recounted their adventures and shown their bruises, the farmers squatted on the sidewalks between occupied houses and demanded to be told what had been happening during the day they had been away.

Some of the woman expected trouble over the coming revelations, and the younger children were shooed away beyond earshot.

Sandy Paris, a fresh-complexioned twenty-five-year-old, would have liked to work out of Big Bend's marshal's office, if they had dared to run their own police force. He wore a distinctive grey shirt, a black leather vest. The brim of his weathered dun stetson was rolled to a point over his long straight nose.

Richy Noakes also preferred trail rider's garb to that of a farmer. He was a few years older, auburn-haired and very muscular. He had a pronounced jaw like his older brother and a rather bony forehead to go with it.

After several promptings, Sandy was the one to speak out.

'You men won't like what I have to tell you. Richy an' me, we were patrollin' in your absence along this near bank of the Big Muddy, keepin' an eye on the comings and goings of the Redman outfit, when we came upon a stranger. He was ridin' from the north an' almost certainly headin' for Redman City.

'We put the glass on him, and then studied him from close up an' sure enough, we recognized him. He was a man we jest couldn't let go through to the Redman's town.'

Jay Paris glanced at his toil-worn wife, and shifted uneasily.

'What is it you're sayin', boy? Get to the point, will you?'

Richy Noakes could not keep quiet. He butted in. 'He was none other than Wilbur Garrotty, the most hated hangman in the whole of the west. You'll see now why we had to waylay him. He was goin' to Redman City, sent for by those who ramrod the town, an' his purpose is to hang those of our friends an' kin languishin' in Redman City jail. Now do you see why we had to intercept him an' bring him along here?'

'Garrotty's here, in town?'

The query came from old Phil Savage, who had strained really hard to hear the exchanges. He was assured that the real Wilbur Garrotty, travelling hangman extraordinary, was cooling his heels in a cell backing on to the town marshal's office.

Upwards of thirty people suddenly took off and went to have a close look at the feared and hated face. This happened five hours before the jaded dappled stallion plodded into town with Rusty asleep on its back and a foam-flecked claybank tagging along behind.

Consequently, the original four farmers were sleeping by the time their deliverer arrived, and Paris' wife and son saw to his pressing needs without informing him about the other remarkable visitor occupying the barred bedroom in the building on Lincoln Avenue.

Blissfully unaware that a new challenge was about to tax his endeavours. Rusty fell asleep in a tidy but otherwise unoccupied house which possessed only the one iron bedstead. Mrs Paris looked in from time to time, but did nothing to curtail his necessary rest.

Every now and then, Wil Garrotty shook the bars of his cell, but the noise he made did not carry to Rusty's quarters.

# 11

Big Bend's council of war took place in the dining room of a dilapidated hotel on Lincoln Avenue at seven p.m. that same evening.

There were some forty adults in the audience, perhaps thirty of them men of mature age. The rest were younger men and a handful of wives. The four farmers who had been to Freedom Falls to collect the wagon were presiding, Clint Noakes acted as chairman.

'Folks, since we came here we've known troubled times. Others have left the area altogether. Some of our friends and comrades are languishing in Redman City jail, simply because they tried to withstand unfair competition from Redman toadies seekin' to take over their businesses. I hate to remind you of our sufferings an' setbacks, but, well, it seems that we have reached a critical period.

'Due to certain happenings, we can expect an all-out attack from Redman City in the very near future. Knowing this, we either organize a general exodus while we still have time in hand, or we dig in and fight.'

All the time he was talking, Noakes' eyes were ranging over the troubled faces in front of him. He paused when he saw Rusty Redman sitting off to his right, separated from the audience and the speakers.

'Before we open up this discussion, I'd like to introduce to you a young fellow called Rusty who lit into the five Redman characters who attacked us. He had to shoot two, an' the other three are in Freedom Falls jail. Folks, meet Rusty.'

There was a storm of hand clapping. Rusty blushed, stood up, toyed with his hat and raised his hand for silence. 'Folks, it's good to make your acquaintance, even in these troubled times. Me,

I've got a personal grievance against the Redmans of Redman City. I've ridden a long way to see the place, thinkin' they were decent folk. Already I've clashed with them twice. I aim to visit Redman City, even as things are, an' I'd be glad if you count me as one of your number in whatever you're plannin' to do.'

He sat down, and Noakes resumed. There was a lot of argument and quite a bit of dissidence. None of the assembled people had a plan to put forward. No one seemed to think they were powerful enough to fight back in force.

Sandy Paris stood up. 'The matter of Wilbur Garrotty is urgent. He's due in Redman City tomorrow. If he doesn't turn up, the Redmans will hang our kin without waitin' for another hangman.'

A man at the back remarked: 'Keepin' Garrotty here is only puttin' off the evil day. Holdin' him against his will is sufficient excuse for them to come over here an' fire the town — or worse!'

The farmers in front were embarrassed. Rusty listened for a few more minutes and then stood up. 'Folks, why don't you substitute one of your number for Garrotty? If you could send in someone not known to the Redmans, maybe the prisoners could be sprung out of jail an' brought back here!'

The sheer audacity of Rusty's suggestion quietened the assembly for a while.

'It's the sort of scheme that appeals to me,' Jay Paris observed. 'Only thing is, most of our men are known to our enemies. In any case, the fellow who went along there would be takin' a terrific chance! I don't see how he could pull it off.'

More argument. No one volunteered. Rusty spoke up. 'I'll have a go at impersonatin' Garrotty, myself, if you want a volunteer!'

Clint Noakes whistled. 'If anyone could do it, you could, Rusty. But his appearance is well known. How could you pass yourself off as him an' hope to get away with it?'

'He is tall an' dark, right? With a lush black moustache an' beard. I could make out I had enemies, that I have had to change my appearance. I could borrow his horse, take his ropes along with me. I believe I could do it.'

'You could borrow his shovel hat, too, Rusty, if his head ain't too big for you!'

Rusty signalled to Clint. 'I'd like a show of hands for those in favour of me tryin' out my plan, if you please?'

The show of hands demonstrated that the entire gathering was in favour. At this point Rusty was on his feet again.

'Very well, I'll make the ride tomorrow. One thing I want to know before we make any preparations. If I manage to get all those prisoners out of the jail and back to this town, will you arm up an' fight?'

After the briefest of pauses, the whole of the audience stood up and answered in the affirmative with a good deal of fist and hand waving and a tremendous amount of noise.

At eight o'clock the following morning, Rusty went around to the cell block with the two Noakes boys. He studied Wilbur Garrotty through the bars quite intently. In fact, the garrulous hangman took exception to being inspected when he was having his breakfast and he hurled his mug, half full of coffee, at the intruders.

His aim was bad, and the hot liquid was easily avoided. Clint Noakes chided the prisoner for his bad manners. Rusty tutted and laughed.

'Mr Garrotty, I am the one chosen to ride into Redman City an' inform them that you've been delayed. Do you have any messages I could take along?'

The hangman glared at him malevolently. After a while, he believed Rusty. 'Jest tell them if they don't come an' get me soon my fee will be doubled!'

His voice was deep and harsh. Rusty listened to it most carefully. He then collected the shovel hat from a stand in the office and tried it on. To his

171

surprise, it fitted him quite well. He glanced at himself in the mirror. It was a stiff hat, low in the crown and with the brim rolled at the sides. His appearance had undergone a complete change.

'What in tarnation are you doin' with my hat?'

'I'm takin' it along with me to prove it's you an' not somebody else,' Rusty explained gently. 'Adios, Mr Garrotty.'

By way of a farewell, the hangman stood up and shook the bars. A moment later, he was alone again.

Outside, Rusty was saying: 'I'll keep to my own clothes, except for the hat. We could have had the suit off his back, but he's bigger than I am round the chest. Go fetch his horse, Sandy. I'll be ready in a few minutes.'

Rusty retired to his room, saw to his pressing needs, and emerged as Sandy returned, riding the big sixteen hands stockingfoot roan. It was a very spirited creature, but it co-operated with a firm rider. After running his hands through the three special rawhide and manilla hanging ropes which Garrotty had brought along with him, Rusty mounted up, took a turn round the block, and paused for a few moments with the entire population fussing round him *en masse*.

'I'll suggest tomorrow for the hangin' day. All bein' well, the jail break will happen after dark tonight. If you folks want something to do while I'm away, it might be a good thing to rig up a few barricades round the important bits of the town. Have a muster of weapons, an' drill yourselves as for an emergency.'

The crowd opened up for him and he cleared town with their hearty cheers ringing in his ears.

He started to have doubts as soon as he was on his own. If only he had had the time to do some scouting in the hostile town before making his vital effort. He had to assume that every man's hand was against him, until he had sprung the prisoners out of jail. He did his best to compose himself. The lonely ride into danger had started.

★ ★ ★

Towards three o'clock in the afternoon, he started to approach Redman City. He had paused for a half hour around noon, but he was once more feeling over-heated and thirsty. He rehearsed what he thought Garrotty's manner would be. He could not match the deepness of the real hangman's voice. He was gambling that none of the key figures in the town had met Garrotty in the flesh.

His mind sought comfort. Glimpses of friendly people appeared in his troubled imagination. He saw again Jeff More, and remembered what he said. 'If you don't like what you see, come away. Don't get involved.' And then there was Laura, a girl who had started her life as a Redman and turned her back on it all. He wondered if he would get back in one piece to see her again, or if he had taken on too much.

Presently, an oldish man on a high piece of ground wide of the town trained a spyglass on him. The message was passed on. As Rusty started towards the buildings, two hard-eyed deputies came riding to meet him, lining up, one on either side.

Rusty eyed them disdainfully. 'You boys go on ahead. I can make it into town. Tell the Mayor that Garrotty has arrived.'

The two riders were alike enough for twins. They each had a small Roman nose, ears which stuck out like flaps, hunched shoulders and short necks. However, one was cleanshaven and the other had a modest brown moustache.

'We're the brothers Ballance, Mr Garrotty. We know you're expected, but all strangers are required to check in with the boss immediately on arrival.'

Rusty glared at the moustached speaker. 'I make my own rules, young fellow. Go and talk to the Mayor, like I said. I'll be takin' liquid nourishment when I find a suitable place.'

He sat back and clamped a hand on his right hip. The deputies backed off, glowering, and acted according to his instructions. Mindful that it might prove difficult for him to inspect the town openly, he kept his eyes on the alert and learned quite a few things in a short time.

Stretched across between two buildings was a banner with three big faces on it. The device read: *Every man is permitted to vote in this free man's city. Decide who you will vote for as Mayor next week. You have three choices.* Under the pictures were the names of the three candidates. Ringo Redman, Harry Redman, and Vic Redman. In smaller letters, the potential voters were reminded that Ringo was the present mayor; that Harry was the town marshal, and Vic, their travelling representative.

Rusty slowed to a halt and regarded the faces very closely. He felt that in so doing he was not acting suspiciously.

Ringo looked to be about forty-five years of age. His lined face was wearing a big grin which thoroughly bunched his heavy features. There was an extra line down his left cheek which looked like a knife scar. He had on a tailored jacket over a shirt and string tie. There was something distinctive about the stetson which made him look more imposing. The grin failed to hide the grim look in the half closed eyes under the encroaching brows.

If anything, Harry looked slightly more handsome. He did nothing to mask his flinty hard eyes and the tightness of his mouth.

The third face gave Rusty cause for grim satisfaction. The travelling representative was out of town. He was the same Vic who had died when more of the hirelings attacked Jabez Burke's place. He, Rusty, was probably the only man in town who knew Vic Redman's exact whereabouts. Unless some scavenging animal had shifted his carcass.

While he had been studying the

banner, countless people had paused on the sidewalks, filled with curiosity about him. Broadly, he figured they could be channelled into two categories. The bold and noisy, who felt they had the confidence of the Redman hierarchy, and the discreet and cowardly who found it best to be unobtrusive and self-effacing.

Further up the street, he was surprised to see a giant cottonwood with a comparatively new tower-like scaffold erection standing underneath a substantial horizontal bough. Obviously, this was the spot where the executions were to take place. There was a trapdoor on the platform some twenty feet above the ground. A length of manilla rope with a noose on the end swung above the structure in the breeze. The rope went up about fifteen feet above the platform, was threaded through a pulley and block attached to the tree branch. From there, the longer part of it was trained down the bole of the tree. The last few feet were coiled round two stout metal pegs driven into the trunk.

Rusty squinted up at the erection from under the big Quaker-style shovel hat. A man could either be hung by the neck through having the trapdoor released beneath his feet, or by someone hauling on the rope from ground level.

He moved on, his head full of disquieting thoughts. Within a few yards, he came across the Big Muddy saloon and angled the big roan towards the hitch rail outside it. Perhaps twenty or thirty men were using the tables and the bar at that time. Rusty stepped purposefully through them and put up four fingers in front of a balding barman.

'Don't ask if I've checked in yet. I'm Garrotty, the boss' guest. I want four fingers of the best whisky, *muy pronto*!'

The barman was so taken aback that his jaw dropped. He reached for the bottle, pushed forward a glass and huskily suggested that the newcomer should measure his own four fingers. Rusty nodded, moved away with the bottle and glass and found himself a vacant table.

He had disposed of the first four fingers and two more when the deputies reappeared and came over to him.

The cleanshaven one touched his hat. 'Mr Garrotty, our present Mayor is the boss, Mr Ringo Redman. Him and his brother usually meet important visitors in the dining room of the City Hotel. If it's all the same to you, he'd like to have you along there to make you welcome.'

Rusty nodded slowly. He gave his bottle and glass to the moustached Ballance and told him to tell the barman to put the reckoning on the boss' account. The deputies were almost stupefied: so was the barman, but no adverse comment was made as the redoubtable 'hangman' left the establishment *en route* for his interview.

* * *

The two ruling Redmans were occupying padded chairs around a circular table in the hotel. Ringo was easily recognizable on account of his heavy brows and the scar tissue. His cream jacket was undone, as was his string tie. He had pushed his grey leather stetson to the back of his head. Ringo removed a cigar butt from his mouth, favoured Rusty with a fixed grin and kicked a chair in his direction.

'Good day to you, Mr Garrotty. Glad you could make it. We were beginnin' to think you'd be late for our big day tomorrow.'

Rusty grinned in his turn. He slowly took off his shovel hat, moved round the table and offered his hand to be shaken. Ringo went through the motions.

A certain amount of basic interest showed in Marshal Harry Redman's hard blue eyes, but no sort of smile softened the small thin line of his mouth. He was about ten years younger than Ringo. He was six feet tall, which made him three inches shorter than the Mayor. His star was pinned to a new grey shirt. The flat-crowned cream stetson worn squarely on his head also looked to be brand new.

The marshal went through the formality of shaking hands. Rusty seated himself. He received a cigar from Ringo, while Harry produced a newspaper cutting from his pocket and handed it over to the newcomer.

With some show of courtesy, Rusty reached for it. On it was an ill-defined photograph of the real Wilbur Garrotty. Bulky clothing, shovel hat and huge amounts of facial hair. Without betraying his uneasiness, Rusty put a match to the cigar, inhaled and then started to chuckle.

'That there picture sure is an old one, marshal. There was a time when practically every man in the western territories knew what I looked like. After two or three attempts on my life, I had to change my appearance. Cut off the facial hair, slim down a little. Wear different clothes. I still have to make a detour or two, now and again, but lookin' different keeps me alive an' in business.'

Rusty chuckled over the cigar until he almost choked.

Harry remarked: 'Bein' careful keeps me in office, Mr Garrotty. Do you have any means of positive identification?'

Rusty slowly sobered down and frowned. 'Well, I have the same horse as I've used for a few years. He's outside. Then there's my ropes.'

He appeared to run out of ideas at that stage. He really was perspiring when he dipped into a pocket of his shirt and brought out the special two-coloured bandanna given to him by Laura all those miles away. At once, the atmosphere changed. Ringo cackled. He reached for it, turned it this way and that, showing the red side and then the black. The Mayor tossed it over for the marshal to inspect.

The marshal again showed impolite interest, but this time he was impressed.

He leaned forward and showed that his own neck cloth had the same distinctive make and colouring. The Mayor produced a third from his side pocket.

'All right, Garrotty, that's all the identification we need,' Ringo remarked.

'Where did you get it?' Harry asked evenly.

'I met a Redman on my travels. A fellow with a face like one of those votin' pictures you have flyin'. I didn't ask any questions, an' he didn't ask me many. But he did recognize me before I stripped off the beard and moustache. I've seen the scaffold. When do you want the hangin' to take place?'

'Tomorrow at ten o'clock. That'll give you time to study the condemned men an' get your plans in order. We have a room for you at the hotel right here. When you've freshened up an' eaten, go along to the cell block, why don't you an' study your victims.'

Ringo guffawed. Harry smirked. Somehow Rusty managed a gusty laugh. It was only when he was alone in his room that he fully realized how much of a strain he had been under.

# 12

The front room on the upper floor of the City Hotel was well ventilated, comfortable and everything Rusty could wish for. After stripping down and taking a wash in the hand basin, he stretched out on the single bed and smoked.

He was troubled about the future, as any man would be in his circumstances. He would need a whole lot of luck if he was to spirit away a dozen men from the cells unnoticed by the partisan Redman locals. Even if they reached Big Bend unharmed, the residents there would have to face up to a pitched battle. Maybe they would live to hate him as much as they did the make-believe Redmans who were causing all the present trouble.

He thought about Ringo and Harry. He felt intuitively that they were not blood brothers. Neither were they kin to Laura Burke. These two were opportunist killers who had moved in upon the old Redman set-up and made it their own.

They ruled by fear, but they could be ousted; provided a sufficient number of people thought it was possible. He could only guess at the number of loyal gunmen willing to take up arms against the general populace on behalf of the ruling officials.

If only the fearful townsfolk could be restored in spirit, the town could be carried for them. Only drastic action, out of which Ringo and Harry could be seen to wilt, would make them militant enough to put matters right.

Around five o'clock he went down to the dining room and ordered a meal. The room was deserted, but obviously the word had gone round as to who he was and how he was to be treated. Having eaten his fill he took the roan along to a livery at the west end of town and asked that it should be put out in the corral at the back with a nose bag on. The liveryman agreed to this move, and the animal joined several others out in the corral. Already, Rusty was thinking about the necessary transport for the prisoners, if he should manage to free them.

Next, he moved leisurely along to the scaffold with his three ropes and climbed to the top. Upwards of fifty people watched him without asking questions. He had in mind changing the existing rope for one of his own, but that — clearly enough — would require some climbing and manoeuvring which might just give away the fact that he was no expert with ropes.

So, eventually, he came away apparently satisfied with the existing rope. He carried beer up to his room and pondered over what he still had to do. After that, he walked along to the marshal's office and asked to see the prisoners.

Harry Redman was just leaving. He turned Rusty over to the Ballance boys, who took down the keys and admitted him to the corridor alongside of the three occupied cells. It was hot in the passage. The small barred windows were highly placed, and admitted very little air.

Four men occupied each cell. Rusty wandered along slowly, eyeing them over and feeling a chill down his spine as the spirited ones stared back at him.

'Any of you men expectin' a reprieve?' he asked bluntly.

Most of the incarcerated men merely stared back at him. Somebody murmured something about who was asking.

Pete Ballance, the moustached deputy, stepped closer to the bars. 'This is Mr Wilbur Garrotty, travellin' hangman, gents. He's travelled quite a long way to do the honours for you at ten o'clock in the mornin'. So speak nicely to him, an' maybe he'll make it easy for you.'

Rusty hoped there was hidden truth in Ballance's words, but he kept his face straight. He remarked: 'The scaffold only takes one at a time. I'll be back here, later this evenin', to see if you have any preference about the order of hangin'. There'll be those among you who don't like waitin', an' others who want to hang on to life until the last possible moment.'

'Do any of you have anything to say to Mr Garrotty right now?' the other deputy queried.

No one spoke, but an unidentified man made a rude noise which infuriated the deputies and caused Rusty to smile inwardly. He re-entered the office, thanked the Ballances for the assistance and left again. This time, he went on a tour of the town, absorbing impressions.

\*     \*     \*

Some time after eight, the town started to get lively. The men in power had passed the word about the coming hanging ceremony and those who openly approved of the Redman cut-throats began to act like it was the eve of a public holiday.

The beer and the whisky started to flow like the fourth of July and, with this change of atmosphere, Rusty's spirits lifted a little. He returned to the peace office a little after nine o'clock and found it occupied only by the veteran jailor, a man who answered to the name of Sailor Please. He was an old seafarer, partially incapacitated by rheumatism. He had a square-cut grey beard, a reefer jacket which had long since seen better days, a straw hat and a handy belaying pin. He seemed surprised when Rusty breezed in and started talking to him as if he was human.

Rusty drank a small whisky which the old man poured out for him. In answer to the question, 'Do you approve of the people in power here?' Sailor said: 'That's a funny question for a visitor to ask. Let's put it this way. I'm too old to go fightin' the bosses at my age. All I want is simple employment an' the right to end my days in peace.'

Together, they drank some more whisky. Rusty elicited from Please that both the Ballance deputies were out on the town, and that Harry Redman hardly ever showed his face in the office after ten o'clock.

'Tell you what I'll do, Sailor. I have some writing to do. I'd like to do it here. You keep workin' on that whisky for a while, an' when the sun goes down I'll come back an' relieve you so that you can go an' live it up yourself. How will that be?'

At first, it sounded far too irregular to the old sailor, but Rusty flashed the unusual bandanna, which the jailor knew about, and mentioned free whisky, if he complied. Sailor had a gargle out of his bottle and Rusty retired, feeling fairly sure that he would get co-operation later.

The time dragged until the shadows appeared, and Rusty wasted ten minutes mentally putting himself into the right mood to commence the operation. Sailor came across the floor, well oiled and quite ready to leave the building in the hangman's care. Rusty handed over the price of a bottle, ascertained that Harry had been in and would not be returning and that the deputies were reputed to be well and truly drunk in a saloon up the street.

'I don't want you to come back before midnight, unless you feel tired. As for the prisoners, I shall advise them to get off to sleep early. So don't disturb them when you do come back. All right?'

Sailor did not grasp the implication that Rusty would not be there when he returned, and presently he slipped out by the front door and ghosted across the street, heading for his favourite drinking place on the south side of the town.

After checking that no one was approaching, Rusty collected the keys and went through to the corridor. 'Now listen, men, an' listen good. Garrotty is a prisoner at Big Bend. I'm here to get you out. The only thing is, everybody has to come, and be willin' to take the risk. Anybody not with me?'

The sleeping men shook themselves awake and stared. Rusty added: 'The Redmans have had one or two setbacks lately, only they don't know about them yet. We have to grab all the horses in the corral at the back of the livery, west end of town, saddles where they are available, an' some guns from here. Now, let's get organized . . .'

Taking all their available belongings, the prisoners trooped out by the rear door, already armed with revolvers and rifles from the office. At the livery, the Redman owner surprised them, but he was quietly suffocated by the prisoner whose business he had taken.

After that, the motley throng moved out towards the west. Only one or two drunks noticed their clandestine progress and they did not realize the significance of it. Four horses were carrying double burdens. This kept down the rate of progress for long after they had reached Redman Creek, a tributary of the Big Muddy.

From there, they turned north, and within half an hour, they were accosted by Sandy Paris, who seemed to rise up out of nowhere. He and Richy Noakes had come along with extra horses. After that, the party made good progress, and the ghost town was achieved in the early hours.

There were joyful reunions. The spirits of the ghost town dwellers were as high as those of the roisterers in Redman City. Rusty entered upon a short discussion with the top men, and retired for a short rest eminently satisfied with the defence arrangements. Lookouts were posted. The residents were militant, and the released prisoners would make themselves useful when they had rested.

★   ★   ★

The alarm must have been given in the early hours, because the riding guns of the pseudo-Redmans appeared within a half-hour of dawn. They grouped up on high ground about half a mile away, and looked down upon the dilapidated township through their spyglasses.

The outfit had turned out in force. Altogether, there were two dozen riders. As usual, the outer buildings showed no signs of life. Even using the spyglasses, the group could not see anything of the barricades and ditches which had been dug around the tenanted streets.

It looked like a push-over for a frontal attack in force, but Ringo and Harry hesitated. They had no clear proof that the escaped prisoners were in the ghost town. In fact, they might be miles away armed with stolen guns and riding stolen horses. The Garrotty business angered them more than anything. Either the hangman had organized the escape, or he had become the prisoner of the escaped prisoners.

It was all very unsatisfactory. The setback meant a possible undermining of Redman authority and, clearly, the more militant hired guns were in need of a blood-letting to restore their confidence.

'Brother,' Ringo remarked, 'it all looks very peaceful, but I think we have to assume our missin' prisoners are in there somewhere.'

'I agree with you, Ringo. Let's ride on down there an' shoot up this part of the town.'

With one Redman at each end, the twenty-four attackers thinned out into line abreast and made their first assault with their tails up and spirits high. There was still no sign of life until the rifles began to fire into them from the 'empty' buildings at a distance of less than fifty yards.

No less than six men and three horses were killed in the primary assault. The attackers fired off a lot of bullets, but they had no clear idea of the casualties in the buildings. Just as Ringo was about to tell his men to retire, two large groups came away without waiting for orders.

Behind a hedge and a scattering of boulders, they took stock of themselves. 'Eighteen men left. Two with minor wounds. Those ghost town folks sure do mean business. We'll have to treat them with more respect in future.' Ringo's voice was scarcely confident.

The discomfited riders did not need the situation spelled out for them. They were up against a goodly number of fighting citizens with their future at stake. None of the attackers could expect any sort of quarter if the day went against them.

\* \* \*

Inside the town, Rusty and the Noakes' went from building to building discussing what might happen next. Jay Paris and his son were holed up in a shack at the southern end of the outer street. Jay remarked: 'When they come again, they'll come like Indians, crawlin', hidin' an' runnin'. What'll we do if they penetrate one of the buildings?'

Rusty grinned. 'We evacuate the building. Let them have it. Put our men behind the barricade dug out at the back, an' throw fire into the building! We can afford to be ruthless with all these unoccupied timbered structures. We sacrifice for a new start. If fire won't put them off, we'll try dynamite.'

He made it sound easy. In fact, he was feeling far more confident since he managed to quit Redman City.

★　★　★

Two hours later, the next attack came. Upwards of half an hour elapsed before any of the crawling gunmen got anywhere near the wooden structures. And then they were pinned down. The defenders conserved their ammunition, although they had plenty, saved up for a long time, against the day.

Early in the afternoon, four men wide on one flank, that nearest the south-west, managed to force their way into a building. Two defenders darted out at the back just before they entered and the third, a stocky farmer, had to dive out of an upper window and run the gauntlet of two accurate guns before he made it behind the barricade.

The defenders behind the barrier turned their fire against the lower windows, and that drove the gunmen upstairs. From the higher angle, their return fire pinned down those behind the barricade. For a few minutes, the situation looked bad. If the attackers got control of that end of the row, it followed that a mounted attack could be launched from the south. Riders might even penetrate behind the carts and barrels, which only covered the nearer half of the town.

It fell to Rusty to do something about the setback. He worked his way out on to a roof behind the barricade and cautiously applied a match to a dynamite stick. He aimed to throw it through an upper window, but his aim was high. And yet his luck was in. The roof it landed on had lost some of its wooden covering. The stick dropped through a hole into the room below.

Defenders in the street systematically pumped shells into the building until it blew apart. The sight and sounds were devastating. One body was hurled high in the air. No one was thought to have survived. Furthermore, the building next in line caught fire. As that spread, defenders further down the outer line prepared to evacuate, but it was the attackers who withdrew for re-grouping.

By early evening all those guns across the west side had crawled away. A lookout on a high building confidently reported that they had all withdrawn to the comparative safety of the dried-out *arroyo* on the north-west side.

Rusty and the defenders were relieved, for a time. Thinking men knew that two factors could improve the Redmans' prospects. The advent of darkness, or reinforcements. Rusty thought they might have to cope with both.

# 13

On a flat roof top fifty yards behind the earthworks and ditch parallel with the dried-out *arroyo*, Rusty and the leading citizens held a parlay at nine in the evening.

'Tonight, friends, might be critical,' Rusty murmured, as he removed the spyglass from his eye, and handed it to Jay Paris.

Sandy remarked: 'But we've done well today, Rusty, you'll allow that. Why, the Redmans can't have much more than a dozen fit men lyin' low there in the *arroyo*. They don't have the numbers to attack us in force. Not as they are now, anyways.'

Rusty patted him on the shoulder. 'I don't want to appear too pessimistic, Sandy, but if they get reinforcements they could infiltrate round the east side of town where we have no barriers, an' that could be the beginnin' of the end for all these decent people. If we can, we have to keep the initiative in some way.'

'You surely wouldn't expect our boys to crawl out there in front of them an' make a shootin' match of it,' Windy Neumann muttered.

'I agree,' Rusty replied. 'We couldn't afford a frontal attack. Nor can we stand any sort of a reverse. We need to keep them on the hop, though. I suppose there's no chance the gully could be flooded?'

The older Paris stroked his moustache, deep in thought. 'Well, the waters sure enough used to flow along there. Until the Redmans made a dam a few miles north. In doin' that they sent the full body of water down the main stream of the Big Muddy which flows past the Circle R. It also deprived us farmers of essential waters for our holdings.'

Richy Noakes started to grin. 'But dams can be blasted, ain't that so, Rusty?'

The dark-haired young man nodded. 'I'd say that sounds like a useful possibility. If we can get some volume of water down the gully before they make a move, that would panic them into doin' something when they weren't ready. In any case, I don't think they'd expect anything like that.'

Clint Noakes started to whistle. 'Well,' he then remarked, 'we do have dynamite, an' there's a big volume of water builds up behind the dam. I'd say it's worth a try.'

The others all signified agreement. 'All right, then, give me two volunteer helpers,' Rusty suggested. 'We'll leave for the dam before dark.'

There was a deal of argument about who should go along with the explosives, and Rusty finally had to make his own choice. He selected Richy and Sandy, who at once went away to run out three horses and make ready the explosives.

At half past nine, the trio mounted up in Lincoln Avenue, exchanged a few last minute observations with the older men who were staying behind, and then slipped quietly away towards the east. By ten o'clock they were well clear of the ghost town and heading north.

All the time they were riding they kept listening for a resumption of gunfire, but it never came.

★  ★  ★

'What time is it, Rusty?'

It was midnight. The trio had just arrived at the dam. They were seated with their legs out of the stirrups, surveying the solid wall of logs which for upwards of two years had been sending the full volume of Big Muddy waters down the main stream. The scudding water was less than a foot below the top level of the dam. The rear of the structure was covered in green moss. Here and there were tiny leaks. In the middle, it was over twelve feet from top to bottom.

Rusty sucked hard on a cigarette.

'I've never blown a dam before, but I'd say we need to strap all our six sticks together an' push them in fairly low on the *arroyo* side.'

'One of us could get down in the gully and light it, an' then skip out,' Richy opined.

'That would be a bit risky, wouldn't it?' young Paris queried.

'I think we couldn't take that risk,' Rusty decided. 'One of you could get down there an' fix the charges, an' then, after you've been hauled out, we could light a long fuse from up here. About fifteen feet would do it, I guess.'

One thing that Rusty liked about working with these young men, they listened to sensible reasoning and did not protest they knew better. Richy slithered down the side of the gully, carrying the sticks and the long fuse. While he was busy, Rusty had another idea.

'If this idea works, we shall want some of our number in behind the Redmans. I figure two of us ought to be on the other bank when the logs go up. The third man could light the fuse on this side, an' be responsible to get back to town in a hurry an' warn our friends to be ready for action.'

Sandy nodded. 'But what if rushin' waters travel faster than a man on horseback?'

The other two saw the good sense behind his remark. The plan was altered so that the pair on the west bank could actually start the fuse. That gave Sandy, on the east bank, a chance to start his return ride before the blast. As soon as young Paris saw the full significance of his part of the action, he was anxious to go.

Rusty shook him by the hand and urged him to leave. 'You'll hear the waters on the move! Don't stop to look at them!'

Sandy waved back and increased the distance between them. Almost at once, Rusty backtracked down the bank on the grey's back, and crossed over, leading young Noakes' buckskin by the reins. Five minutes later, Richy came up from below and handed over the loose end of the fuse.

'You ready to move off, pardner?' Rusty asked patiently.

Nodding vigorously, the other hurriedly forked his buckskin and rode off down the bank side. When he was fifty yards away, Rusty removed the butt of his cigarette from his mouth and applied it to the fuse. Almost at once, it spluttered into life. He knew a feeling of great exhilaration as the spluttering fuse moved slowly down the bank, absorbing the long length of the wire, inch by inch.

For the first time in the long series of brushes with the Redmans he had the feeling that the renegades' power was on the way out. Some distance away, Richy Noakes called hoarsely. Rusty knew that there was no point in watching what he took to be the inevitable explosion from close up. In fact, he might be inviting an accident.

He gave the grey a touch of the rowel

and off they went in the wake of the buckskin. The two of them had covered a hundred yards when their unbearable curiosity made them rein in and wait to see the big explosion.

As they stared into the gloom behind them, the spluttering fuse was no more significant than a firefly. Foliage blotted it out from them for a time. They almost held their breath. At last, the earth seemed to shudder. A deep rumble followed at once. The horses reared and plunged as the end of the dry watercourse was suddenly illuminated in bright orange light, tinged with red.

An indescribable noise followed, like a huge unseen animal in torment. Logs were blasted upwards and outwards. Smaller pieces of wood were hurled along the gully beside them. Gurgling sounds preceded the first surge of turbulent water as it heaved through the lower part of the breached wall.

And then the water tumbled past them at the very bottom of its former course. At first, they thought it would soon outstrip them, but the ground was incredibly dry and much of the initial volume of water was sucked into the earth. An unworldly sizzling sound accompanied the new movement. They stared at one another for a minute more, found nothing to say to each other, and then they were riding, moving as fast as they safely could over the rough unbroken ground.

\* \* \*

At one o'clock in the morning, Jay Paris, Clint Noakes, Neumann and old Savage were among those who had relieved others in the ditch behind the earthworks facing the arroyo. Morale was low, due to the unearthly hour and the uncertainty of the waiting.

Paris remarked: 'Folks do say that no news is good news, but I don't know. The Redmans have been reinforced, even if only by a handful of men, an' there's no signs of our trio. Maybe they were ambushed on the way. What do you boys think?'

'It's a long way to the dam, Jay,' Clint pointed out. 'I doubt if the water will get here quickly. Besides, one or two of the boys claim they heard a loud thump some time back. At least we haven't been attacked while they were away.'

★   ★   ★

Savage, cut off from the others by his deafness, whistled tunelessly.

In the *arroyo*, Jack Ballance, who had ridden to town to collect reinforcements, was trying to explain to Ringo why his mission had all but failed.

'It wasn't easy, Ringo. Practically everybody had gone to bed. When I clanged on the cleaver there was a very poor response. One or two men got up and argued that their ridin' horses were missin' from the livery, which was true, I suppose. Others stayed well out of sight. I would have stayed longer and tried a bit of old-fashioned persuasion, but I thought you might be in difficulties here, so I had to come to a decision.'

Ringo ripped off two or three vicious oaths. Men who knew him well eased further away from him, fearful of his temper. Someone a few yards away from them whispered a warning of sorts.

'Your brother went off up the gully some time ago, Jack. See if you can find out what's happened to him!'

Inwardly very relieved, the deputy moved off, hoping for some news to lift the spirits of his leaders. He kept scrambling up the soft sandy soil until he came to the very last man at the northern end of the offensive line. He squatted down beside the other man, catching at his breath.

'What goes on, Dixie?' he asked hoarsely.

'Your brother is up there a piece. He called back to me a minute or so ago. Thinks there's a rider on his way into the town, comin' from the north. Some

212

sort of a messenger. Maybe we'll know something in a minute.'

Presently, the well known sounds put up by a horse and rider carried to them. It was difficult to tell how far he was away, or how fast he was travelling. While they waited, tensed and straining hard to hear well, a rifle boomed suddenly some fifty yards away.

There was a sharp cry from the direction of the ridden horse. Pete Ballance's familiar voice called out: 'I think I winged him! Don't let him get away!'

The rifle erupted flame again, and soon Dixie and the other Ballance had joined in. They were firing in the dark, with only the sounds to guide them. Upwards of six bullets were fired. When their ears had stopped singing, they heard the hoof sounds again, only more distantly.

Jack Ballance stayed where he was, not knowing what he should report to the Mayor. His brother came back with his smoking shoulder gun shortly afterwards. It was clear that he thought the rider was wounded, but that he had managed to go on by.

The Ballances moved back down the line. What the twins had to say merely fanned the fury of the Mayor and the town marshal. Harry Redman kicked the low-built fire and muttered: 'We've got to do something, take some form of offensive action, Ringo. Something. Whatever it is!'

'My sentiments exactly,' Ringo replied heatedly. 'I don't intend to be pinned down in this stinkin' river bed for much longer. Have the boys boost the fire, an' light those torches.'

Harry moved away to implement the order.

★  ★  ★

Sandy Paris had been desperately unlucky to be hit by the Ballance bullet when he was so close to home. He had sustained a very useful pace all the way from the dam. His natural exuberance

214

and reckless lack of fear had finally betrayed him. Instead of detouring well away from the gully, as the trio had done on the way out, he had casually diverged from it without actually ascertaining how far north it was occupied by the enemy.

The bullet which hit him had ripped into his chest under the right arm. Within seconds, he knew that he had a fatal wound. The finality of such a setback often speeds the action of the brain. In Sandy's case he only wanted sufficient time to get back to his friends and give them the startling news.

Sheer dogged determination kept him in the saddle until his mount, a sturdy pinto, had carried him as far as the north-eastern outskirts. There, he slipped sideways and sagged to the ground. He saw a frightened boy's face without actually recognizing the person.

'Tell my father the water's comin' real soon. Rusty an' Richy, they're on the other side of the *arroyo*, in behind the enemy. Tell them ... tell my father — '

Bubbled blood welled out of the side of his mouth, his energies ran out and he flopped, leaving the startled youth feeling outraged, with his mouth wide open.

Giving a sharp cry, the lad drew attention from the nearest building, where his mother and uncle were sharing a lookout position. They were out in a few seconds and crouching over the limp body. Before they could do anything to reduce the shock in the boy, he had taken to his heels, running towards the earthworks, where Jay Paris was known to be.

Total disregard for his safety, or for keeping quiet, drew a probing rifle shot from the gully, but he ran on unscathed, until Jay Paris, himself, dragged him down and refused to listen to him until he had recovered his breath.

'Sandy is back. He's hit. He — he died, but he gave me a message, Mr Paris.'

The farmer was badly shaken. He retired from the line and left others to figure out the purport of the message, the delivery of which had been his son's last effort. The loss of young Paris curbed the feeling of optimism which the news engendered. Two other men had died, earlier, on the previous day. Others were wounded. But Sandy Paris was one of the up and coming young men who could have made a name for himself in a brighter future.

The occupants of the trench behind the earthworks waited with mixed feelings. Why had the water not reached them before this?

There was little time for conjecture, because directly Ringo Redman's positive diversion began. A flaming torch sailed through the air like a silent firework. It dropped in the bottom of the trench, and singed the coat of a man who was stretched out there on his back.

Others followed, backed by harrowing cries for vengeance.

# 14

'Your time is nearly up, you ghost town bums!'

Here and there behind the earthworks, flickering shadows showed where the flaming torches had landed. The startled defenders were trying hard to put them out, to keep them away from their ammunition and anything combustible.

Ringo, the one who had shouted the disquieting words, signalled to his men to fire. Gun flashes and the crackle of rifles rattled up and down the arroyo, enough to take the heart out of any sort of opposition. Especially when kept in suspense like the Big Bend people were.

Harry Redman was chewing on a piece of tobacco, carefully keeping his nerves in check. He was waiting for the signal to advance out of the gully, up the slope to the earthwork. He thought the order to go was overdue.

The man next to Ringo asked a question.

'No, let them stew in their own juice for a few minutes. If their nerves are jumpy they won't be able to shoot straight, an' that'll be a good thing for us!'

Harry was often critical of Ringo's handling of men. On this occasion, his impatience made him speak out. 'Do we go on wastin' ammuntion, then?'

Ringo glared at him, and signalled for a temporary cease fire.

At the same time, the faintest of ground shocks came along the gully, causing the men hunkered down there to stare at one another. In groups of twos and threes, they whispered together, clearly unable to think why the ground was shaking. No sort of subsidence had ever been known in the area. Why should it happen now when they were contemplating an attack on the ghost town by night? Could the inhabitants of Big Bend have had anything to do with it? The gunmen remembered the riding messenger who had ridden down from the north. What if he could have performed some act of sabotage?

No one came remotely near to guessing what, in fact, had happened.

Pete Ballance came down the line of guns, breathing through his moustache. His hips and knees were aching due to his half-crouched way of travelling. As soon as he arrived between the tensed-up leaders he forgot the words with which to frame his fears.

'What is it?' the marshal snapped at him.

Thinking he was referring to the earth shaking, Ballance shook his head. 'I really don't know, marshal. There was a big thump some time back, and now this — this earth rumbling. I can't make out what it is, but it's troublin' me.'

'Have a guess, you fool!' Ringo prompted fiercely.

Even in the dark, the deputy could

read the tension in his leaders' faces. He reminded himself that his own safety depended upon their intelligent planning; also the life of his brother.

'All I can think is that we are in the bed of an old stream, a tributary of the Big Muddy. Is it possible there's water further up the gully an' comin' this way?'

Harry pushed him aside. 'What do you think, Ringo?'

'It's jest possible, Harry. The ghost town folk have been up to something. What can we do if the waters come? Do you think they'd really have the nerve to blow the dam?'

'If we don't make a move, we might have to take an unofficial swim,' Harry commented, without humour.

'And if the waters come, do we go forward, or backward?'

'Shucks, Ringo, are we runnin' this part of the county, or is it runnin' us?'

Ringo grinned unexpectedly. 'That's what I thought you'd say, brother.' He filled his lungs. 'All you men stand by to give them another fusillade!'

The sounds of levering were fading as the first trickle of water carried as far as the Redman party.

Dixie shouted: 'Hey, Boss! I got water round my feet, an' my face is gettin' splashed! Why can't we get a move on?'

The Redmans waited long enough to confirm what Dixie had said, and then they had no alternative. Thin probing trickles of water were squirming and hissing through them as the next order was given.

'*Fire!*'

The flashes, the jerks against the shoulders, the crack of bullets being ejected. The anxious attackers were busy again.

'*Everybody up, out an' over!*'

At last, Ringo had contrived to raise the words which Harry had been waiting for. One after another, the men moved. They kept low, crawling and wriggling and hoping that they would not be cut down before they got as far as the formidable earthworks up from the *arroyo*.

For a minute or two, no retaliatory fire troubled them. The defenders were listening. Due to their position they were a little later in knowing about the trickle of water building up in the river bed. The closer proximity of the *arroyo* guns finally warned them of the sneak attack. Men began to fire back again, using gun slits deliberately fashioned out of the earthworks against just such an occasion.

Jay Paris was back by this time. He had used his bereavement to spur him on to aggressive action. Scheming alone, he had sent a man round the north end of the ditch and earthworks to fire into the attackers from the flank. Similarly, another armed man had placed himself at the other end, balancing on a high point of the barricade.

'All right, boys? Take your time an' make your shots count! The waters are comin' down the *arroyo* again! By next week, we'll be usin' the stream to feed our fields an' livestock! So hit 'em hard! They've got no proper place to retreat into!'

Twenty men struggled forward out of the stream bed, including two with leaking wounds and others with grazes. Darkness to some extent cut down upon the casualty rate. As the distance between the crawling men and the mound of earth lessened, three attackers were eliminated, along with one defender hit in the chest with a ricochet.

Paris retired to the nearest house, mounted to a level which made marksmanship easier, and began to probe the gunmen from there. The night air was filled with the harsh snap and crackle of gunfire, the stench of smoke and the cries of men bent upon the destruction of others.

Marshal Harry Redman suddenly rose from the ground and sprinted up the uneven slope of the earthworks. He hurled his empty rifle down upon the defenders below him and whipped out his matching .44 Colt revolvers. Silhouetted in the faint light, he paused momentarily to give other, faint-hearted attackers, a boost in courage. He was just starting to pump bullets down into the dirt trench when another, fired from an entirely unexpected direction hit him high in the back and threw him forward into the ditch.

His dramatic exit gave Ringo a few seconds of panicky conjecture, but the attack had to go on. Behind them, the foaming waters were very slowly gaining depth, and looking as if no force on earth would stop them any more.

An idea by Windy Neumann paid off here. He had prepared torches, too. He gave an order and that resulted in the flaming brands being tossed in among the crawling attackers. They disturbed the Redman faction, and showed them up to the defenders.

★　★　★

Rusty Redman stood quite still beside a tree bole on the west side of the arroyo. He was breathing hard and trying to come to a decision about the immediate future. Garrotty's shovel hat had long since been discarded. Now, his own big flat-crowned stetson was stuck to his forehead with perspiration. His teeth were clenched in an unusual grimace for him. His Winchester repeater, the weapon which had eliminated the Redman marshal, was angled across his chest, still giving out a wisp of smoke.

Richy Noakes was on the other side of the tree, straining to see the action in the darkness and awaiting instructions.

'They'll never back off into the stream now,' young Noakes yelled hoarsely. 'It must be a foot deep or more!'

Rusty nodded without answering. He was doing his best to assess the situation. Any reckless move on their part could undo their present advantage. At their backs were a score of horses, pegged out in the trees.

Richy's restlessness was getting on Rusty's nerves. 'Hey, Richy, take a look among those horses. Make absolutely sure they don't have a horse minder at our backs!'

If the attackers managed to swarm over the earthworks and capture the trench anything could happen in the hand to hand fighting which would surely follow. For a time, the issue hung in the balance.

In three places guns were blazing away from the upper storeys of buildings. Here and there, a man reached the top of the earth. It was not easy to tell if he slid down the other side alive, or whether he was eliminated by the locals.

Two minutes later, Noakes was back beside him, starting him.

'Nobody at our backs. This side of the stream is ours! Look, they're fallin' back!'

'Sure! If I've read this properly, they'll not stay in the water! They'll come straight across and mount up!

This is where we have to do our stuff, Richy! Keep down low, an' pick your targets carefully!'

Thirteen or fourteen men suddenly broke and turned tail. Down they came towards the gully. The nearest hesitated, seeing the swelling width of the moving water below them. Others pushed up close. Men began to jump down.

Kneeling, and about five yards apart, Rusty and his partner began to line up their weapons. At first, the shooting was infrequent. Soon, the boots of the retreating faction were in the water. They had to look down and wade slowly, or lose their footing. Mindful of all the trouble the Redmans had caused, Rusty deliberately held back. The gunmen must not be allowed to cross. Clearly, they were desperate. If they managed to cross over and retire on horseback, they would live to fight another day.

The water was up to the knees of the foremost.

The dark-haired young man blinked

as his straining eyes picked out the distinctive headgear of Ringo. During the time of his power, Ringo Redman's grey leather stetson had made him stand out among other men. On this tricky occasion, he still stood out.

Rusty lined up on him, licked his lips, steadied his weapon and squeezed. Ringo staggered and almost lost his balance. A man following behind helped to keep him upright in the water. Richy's gun banged, and another gunman slipped backwards and disappeared from sight, his hat floating away from him as another struggled to avoid him and keep moving forward.

In no time at all, the whole of the Redman outfit was in the stream. Some continued to wade through the encroaching tide of water, while others strove to fire back at the two lethal guns on the west bank.

Two more men went down. Others tried to cower in the stream. Men sprang up on to the earthworks and poured further bullets into their backs.

'Drop your guns!' Rusty ordered.

His voice was hoarse. In the cacophony of sound, not many heard it, but within seconds rifles and six guns were discarded into the waters, where they disappeared from sight.

Rusty and his partner stopped firing at once. From the other bank, the spasmodic shooting carried on for perhaps two minutes. As the sound of the last shell echoed into the distance, Jay Paris and others appeared on top of the earthworks.

'Everything all right over there, Rusty?'

'Sure, Jay! Let's have some lamps! When you're ready, we'll be sendin' the survivors back up your side. Make sure you have a suitable reception committee waitin' to take them away!'

Rusty sounded tired, but quite calm. The wounded Ringo, and ten other men, three of whom were also wounded, waited with their hands raised in the deepening stream. The water was up to most men's waists. The

230

non-swimmers were only slightly less fearful of the water than the reception they would get in Big Bend.

Eventually, four lamps were rigged on top of the earthworks. Eight men in all, fully armed, came forward to superintend the prisoners.

'Ready when you are, Rusty!'

Putting aside his hot Winchester, Rusty drew his colt and stepped forward. 'All right, you men, turn around an' make your way out on the other side. Anybody who wants to be awkward gets a lead pill. You'll find the town has plenty of facilities for unexpected guests. Now, move!'

Ringo paused with only one arm raised. 'That's the voice of Garrotty, the hangman! I'd know it anywhere!'

Richy Noakes brought forward their two horses. Rusty mounted up again before making any sort of reply. As he walked the grey forward, he managed to chuckle. 'Not Wilbur Garrotty, Ringo. I was jest his substitute. You'll be interested to know my real name, however. Russell Redman. Known as Rusty to my friends. I'm a *true* Redman! That's more than you will ever be able to say!'

His voice had carried. Some of his supporters and friends were even more surprised than his enemies.

# 15

Due to their losses in fighting to secure their town against the old Redman faction, the ghost town people were not keen to celebrate straight away. The first thing they did was to secure the prisoners and place a regular guard on them.

After that, substantial breakfasts were provided for all, and those not on guard duty had a few hours of sleep. Around nine o'clock in the morning, the youngest and the fittest all bathed in the recently flooded creek. Clint Noakes called a meeting in the square, and Rusty was invited to address the gathering.

In simple language, he explained how he had left his home in Wichita, shortly after his folks departed for England: how he had ridden steadily towards the southwest, hoping to link up with the famous Redmans of Redman City. Clashes with Redman factions on the way were briefly touched upon. He mentioned his meeting with Laura Burke and the subsequent clash near Jabez Burke's cabin, and then the incident in Freedom Falls district where he had chanced upon the farmers from the ghost town being harassed by another Redman group.

Gradually, he explained, his attitude towards the rulers of Redman City had changed. He supposed that he had been prompted to fight those who had brought the name of Redman into disrepute because of some sort of pride in his own surname.

He went on: 'I'm glad my own efforts coincided with the hour of your peril, an' that Big Bend, from now on, can count itself a free town, no longer harassed by bullyin' gun totin' enemies.'

At this stage, a great uproar caused through cheering and hand clapping temporarily halted his speech. For fully five minutes, the relieved people gave vent to their enthusiasm and Rusty had to sit down on the steps of the building behind him until they were finished.

'Thank you, folks, for your show of kindness. As for the future, my self-imposed mission cannot be considered finished until Redman City is restored to its own rule, an' the Circle R ranch has been visited to ascertain the true state of affairs.

'Many of you will want to stay behind to bury your dead, but I'd like to ask for a few volunteers to side me as I return to Redman City with the prisoners. We have to be sure there aren't any more of the old faction strong enough to restore the kind of control that Ringo and Harry enforced. So, I'd like to ask your views on what I've said.'

Jay Paris, sobered by the loss of his son, but still a powerful man when it came to swaying public opinion, stood up to answer.

'We appreciate all that you've told us

about your own personal circumstances, Rusty. I agree about goin' on to Redman City an' the ranch. In my view, the Noakes brothers, Clint an' Richy ought to go along with you, an' Harvey Prole.

'Harvey was one of the men you broke out of jail. He had his saddler's business taken over by a Redman puppet, so he has business to settle. Besides, Harvey was at one time the Mayor. Folks might want him to stand again.'

The Noakes brothers were quite willing to go along with Rusty, who approved of Paris' choice. Harvey Prole introduced himself, and Windy Neumann also offered to go along with the party. Five other men who had been dispossessed joined the group, and half a dozen men of Big Bend volunteered to go along as guards.

At ten o'clock the unusual procession of mounted prisoners and guards started out from Big Bend on their way to Redman City. Ringo Redman and the three other wounded men had been patched up. Eleven survivors in all of the thirty Redman hirelings and supporters who had ridden out to recover the escaped prisoners and at the same time had been intent upon demolishing all resistance in the ghost town.

Wilbur Garrotty, with his ropes restored to him, was permitted to ride at the rear of the column between two guards.

*   *   *

Fifty yards ahead of the column, at one p.m., Rusty Redman headed into the town alone. Here and there, chastened townsfolk gathered together and cautiously watched him. He had changed the horse and the hat, but to them, he was still the hangman who had come into town and mysteriously quit again, at the same time as the prisoners were spirited away.

Sailor Please was one of those who at once recognized Rusty's authority. He dashed away to clang the cleaver, so as to draw a crowd into the big square. Everybody knew that the town was denuded of Redman guns: that the men with authority had ridden out towards the ghost town and not returned.

The population of the township assembled slowly, not at all sure what to expect. As they came, so the slow procession headed up the main street and came to a halt on the open patch to one side of the cottonwood and the scaffold. Very rapidly, the word went round that Ringo Redman and all the feared ones who were with him were prisoners.

The Noakes boys ordered the prisoners to dismount. Ringo and his boys were made to sit in a ring. Their mounts were taken away. The guards made a wider ring around them, and the townsfolk, thirsty for information, crowded closer.

Rusty, who had a sense of occasion, mounted the steps of the scaffold for the second time. There was a lot of peering up, and shading of eyes.

'Folks,' he began, 'the old order of rule by fear in this town is over. Ringo, who never was a true Redman, is before you wounded. The man who called himself Harry Redman is dead. So are the two boys who were his deputies, the Ballances.

'The men you can see before you are the sole survivors of the bullyin' gun totin' outfit who rode out of here. Big Bend is no longer in fear of anybody. It is restored. The dammed up creek is flowin' again. It is time for you to set your town in order.

'Your man, Harvey Prole, is volunteerin' as temporary Mayor. I'm offerin' you Clint Noakes as a temporary town marshal, an' his brother, Richy, as deputy. As soon as I've finished talkin' I want you to go away from here, an' find me a lot of wooden stakes. We're goin' to build a compound right here in this square to house the prisoners.

'The ones you decide have committed crimes for which they should die won't be goin' very far from here, after this.'

He paused and thumped the rail of the scaffold with the flat of his hand.

'Do you approve of Harvey Prole as your temporary Mayor?'

A great chorus of 'Yes', from the loosened tongues, confirmed the appointment. The same thing happened when the names of the Noakes' were offered. While men were away collecting the stakes and tools, Rusty added a few extra items.

'If anybody has wrongfully dispossessed you of your property, leave this assembly an' drag them here. Put them in with the other prisoners! Go an' claim what is rightfully your own!'

A furious hunt ensued. About eight men, all who had misappropriated property in the town, were dragged into view by people they had always taken to be craven cowards. The work of rigging up the compound began. As soon as it was completed, the prisoners were secured by ropes to other stakes near the middle. They stayed there as a constant reminder that the old Redman power was gone.

The Noakes boys organized the guards into watches, and then listened to small complaints and problems put to them by long-suffering people. Rusty made a tour of the town with Prole, Neumann and one or two interested businessmen.

Garrotty followed them as far as the hotel, and there he asked permission to fall out and relax. He gave his word he would not leave town until permission was given and, with that, Rusty lost interest in him. Rusty moved rather wearily towards the peace office.

Sailor Please dusted off the marshal's chair for him, having already digested the public revelations in the square.

'Do I lose my job, now the old Redman gang has fallen?'

'I reckon it depends on how you act in the future, old timer.'

Rusty made a tour of the office, inspected the weapons on the walls, and finally subsided into the big swivel chair formerly occupied by Harry Redman. He gestured for Sailor to take a seat. The latter did so, but not before he had produced a bottle and poured for the two of them.

'Sailor, ghost town is cleaned up. Redman City will set itself to rights in the next day or two. I've got one more port of call. The Circle R ranch. I don't know how I shall find things when I get there. I have it in mind to take along a few hard workin' cowpunchers, if they can be found, and to bring back some other men who favoured the Redman gang too much.'

The old man chuckled and tugged at the ends of his square beard. His watery eyes were alight with sudden interest. He made a few dents in his chair leg with the belaying pin which was almost always with him.

'It can be done. There is a nephew of mine, name of Slim. He cut out from the ranch when the real Redman boys quit. Couldn't hit it off with Bart

McHenry an' the new boys he brought along. Slim's been workin' as a blacksmith in town, but he'd go back to ranch work like a shot if he knew Old Ma Redman was back in charge!

'Besides, he knows the other cow nurses round about who pulled out from time to time. If I passed him the word, he'd round 'em up for you!'

'Make it a priority job, Sailor. Tell him I want to leave within the hour.'

The old nautical man went out at once. He was back in ten minutes with his nephew Slim Please. Slim was in his early thirties; anything but slim. His barrel chest blended in with a large abdomen held in by a broad leather belt. His jowl was relatively firm. His voice was high-pitched for so large a character.

'I hear tell you want men to go back to the Circle R to work, mister. I'm willin' to go myself, an' I've put the word round for certain other fellows I know. I can tell you that the Redman foreman, the one backed up by Ringo an' Harry an' Vic, is away right now.

'But he's due back any time, with the pay-roll for a herd he took up to Colorado.'

'All right, Slim, you'll be goin' along with me, an' stayin' if Ma Redman approves of you. Go an' rustle up your friends, an' make sure they're well mounted.'

\* \* \*

The Circle R was well planned out. Strategically placed around a big low house with large galleries were a bunkhouse, a cookhouse, a smithy, two stables, a large corral and three barns.

Three old hands were tossing horse-shoes in front of the house as Rusty and his small group rode through the paddock a little after six o'clock that same evening. The game stopped as soon as the riders were observed. Rusty nodded to the players and walked the grey across the open ground until he was under the front gallery.

The woman knitting in the rocker was a lean hard-faced female in her early sixties. She had suffered much in her life. She had often said that there were no more surprises in store for her this side of the grave. Without looking down at the riders she glanced sharply at her daughters who were making garments further along the gallery.

'Are you Redman scum, or decent visitors?'

Slim Please and the other riders gasped. Mrs Redman paused in her knitting long enough to nervously push back her greying hair, which was parted in the middle and drawn back in a hard line.

'I'm a true Redman, not one of the gang you fear, Mrs Redman. I've travelled hundreds of miles to make your acquaintance. All the way from Wichita, Kansas.'

The old lady made no sign to show she had heard. Please and the other riders were greatly surprised. The two Redman daughters, later introduced as

Mary and Alicia, stared but only showed hostility.

Please said: 'Mrs Redman, you'll remember me, Slim Please. I can tell you that Big Bend is not a ghost town any more. The creek is flowin', too. And all the Redman gang has been defeated in a gun battle up Big Bend way. Harry Redman is dead. Ringo is wounded and a prisoner in town. Won't you listen to this fellow? He's only come to do you a good turn!'

Mrs Redman appeared to have completely lost heart. 'I heard tell Bart McHenry is due back here at this very minute with the cash for the last delivery of beeves. Get back to town before he shoots you to doll rags, why don't you?'

Rusty whistled, in spite of himself. 'The other Redman, the one called Vic is dead. Your daughter, Laura, approves of me. So do her friends, an' all the folks in Big Bend. Can't you understand? Your fortune has changed for the better!'

The spinster Redman girls were not too old to react. Mary, who was about thirty-six, had a broad jaw and cheekbones, and a bony figure. Her complexion was sallow, her hair lacked lustre, but there was still some feeling showing in the eroded eyes.

The second daughter, Alicia, had green eyes, a high forehead and freckles, but she, too, looked under-nourished.

Rusty was thinking how intensely glad he was that Laura had made it away from this mausoleum of a place before the tyrannical atmosphere got her down. From the rear, a Mexican maid appeared, to whisper in the mistress's ear.

The three old hands knew what it meant. They cleared off, made themselves scarce. Mrs Redman stood up. 'We're goin' in now, Mr Redman. McHenry and the other scum have been seen. There's still time to clear off to town in one piece.'

Rusty felt insulted. He could only guess at the way such a woman had suffered to have all the hope knocked out of her. As the three women gathered up their knitting and materials a sudden feeling of belligerence attacked the dark-haired young man.

'You three don't believe in miracles. Why don't you stay there? Maybe you'll see one.'

Rusty turned to his fellow riders. 'Take your mounts off round the back of the bunkhouse. You can wait inside for the 'punchers. I want them disarmed, if possible, an' taken back to town to face a short sharp trial.'

Mary Redman spoke up for her mother. 'You don't understand! He'll taunt us with the money which he won't hand over. It isn't pretty to watch!'

'Tell your mother that if he has to die, it is better his blood stains the dirt out here, rather than the carpets an' floor within.'

The younger woman, Alicia, gasped and was near to tears. Mary entered the house and came back with her mother, who had thrown a black shawl around her thin shoulders. One after another, they took their seats again.

The old woman said: 'Young man, I heard tell Laura was married. Are you her husband?'

'No, Laura is a widow, but she may not stay that way for long.'

The thundering of hooves came across from the northwest. Seven riders, headed by a big bulky full-figured character in a green and red checkered shirt, entered the home buildings in a cloud of dust, and only reined in when they were in front of the building.

Bart McHenry had a flat whisky bottle stuck in his belt. He had been imbibing. With one hand he gripped the strap of the leather money bag. The other was busy with a big cigar.

'Good day to you, dear Mrs Redman. Here we all are, back in one piece, with the money!'

He kneed his white stallion in beside the dappled grey and clumsily dropped to the ground. 'Who — who's is this crow bait on the house hitch rail?'

Rusty, this far unobserved, stepped forward. 'It's mine. By the way, I'm Russell Redman. I'll be takin' over the money bag this trip. Mr McHenry, I believe?'

There had been a lot of hooting and shouting as the six hired hands in various states of inebriation, manoeuvred their horses in front of the bunkhouse. They dismounted and would have surrounded McHenry and the stranger, but the foreman waved them back. They backed off a short way and lined up to watch the proceedings in front of the cowpunchers' quarters.

A man with a nasal accent asked: 'Who in hell is this jasper, Bart?'

'Claims to be a Redman. Claims to be takin' over the money.'

The new arrivals howled and hooted and threw themselves about. Rusty found it in him to laugh with them. The three women on the gallery were pent up with anxiety.

'Ringo is wounded and a prisoner. Harry was killed last night. Vic was bumped off many days ago. Now, are you goin' to hand over Mrs Redman's money, intact, to me, or do you want to be a martyr?'

A big frown spread over the foreman's lined full face. He took a quick swig out of his liquor bottle and tossed it aside. Large hands adjusted the waist belt, gun belt and the twin holsters.

'What is that martyr talk, stranger? I think in a roundabout sort of way you're askin for a gun showdown. Am I right?'

Rusty nodded. 'Either that, or you turn in your guns an' go into town as a prisoner with the rest of the Redman scum. By the way, if you do decide to shoot it out, hadn't you better discard the money bag? It might interfere with your draw.'

McHenry roared with rage. He hauled the strap over his head and dropped the satchel to one side. 'Hell an' tarnation, this crazy hombre has had more to drink than *I* have, or something! I'm ready when you are, stranger!'

'It might be a good thing if your men didn't stand right there behind you, in case they get hit,' Rusty advised.

After that, he had finished clowning. He felt himself tensing up inside, and he wondered what manner of man he had turned into to be forcing a renegade killer into trading lead. The sun was well over to westward. Its rays were directly in the eyes of McHenry, but Rusty never considered moving around to give him a better chance.

McHenry stood with one hand spread on each side of his massive chest. The Redman women appeared to shrink into themselves. Rusty murmured a thoroughly insulting remark about the demise of the Redman scum.

His words had the effect of further angering the baffled foreman. McHenry gave an angry roar as he dipped for his twin guns. From a promising crouch, Rusty also dipped for his holster. Mrs

Redman cried unheard.

Up came the guns. The foreman's powerful forearms swung up his gun muzzles as if he had been drilled to it. Rusty blinked and fired his .45 as the muzzle was still rising along the line of his opponent's trunk. The three gun shots all merged into one. Rusty felt something touch him on the shoulder. He spun about and dropped. It was his gun shoulder, but the gun still pointed the way he wanted it aimed and he continued firing from a prone position.

McHenry, hit in the chest from the first bullet, had stepped back a pace. His eyes were wide open, as he continued firing with both weapons. His bullets were aimed at the same trajectory, as if his enemy was still standing.

He fired so quickly that both cylinders were empty before he sank down with a second bullet through his left thigh. Ten out of his twelve shells had homed into the wall of the blacksmith's shop. McHenry rocked for a few seconds on his right thigh like a drunken squire awaiting the accolade. And then he slipped over with a gentle expression of bewilderment materially altering his face.

Oddly enough, from his prone position, the first thing Rusty did was to chuckle. His tremendous bluff had paid off. He promised himself that it would be a long time before he talked his way so close to death again. Moving as if he had aged, he clambered to his feet, wandered across to the money satchel and picked it up.

'See what I mean, you ex-Circle R hands? The money goes into *my* possession.' He moved across to the rail in front of the gallery and put his back against it. Raising his voice, he called: 'Okay, now, you new hands! It's time to show yourselves!'

The six momentarily stunned cow-punchers stared at one another and then round about them, as if other men were likely to rise out of the earth. At once, Slim Please appeared at one corner of the bunkhouse. Another man showed at the other end. Yet a third moved into view at the door. The rest of the new arrivals appeared at the windows. All of them had revolvers in their hands.

'This is the last time you six are likely to be seen armed on Circle R territory. Drop your guns before we have to shoot you as well.'

He waited for them to comply. As soon as they had done so, the six new hands moved out into the open and collected the weapons.

'You men will be goin' into town presently. If anyone has a charge to bring against you, the chances are you'll be hung, or put in jail. It ain't likely you'll be found innocent, but if you are, grab your horses an' ride like your lives depend on it. Is that understood?'

No one replied, but there was some nodding. Leaving Slim Please to control the prisoners, Rusty turned his back on them and stalked up on to the gallery. Mrs Redman had already gone indoors, along with Alicia. Mary stayed behind to escort him.

He removed his hat, sat down in the living room and submitted to having a light bandage put round his right upper arm and shoulder. Fortunately, he had suffered only the lightest of burns. The flesh had puckered, giving him some pain. Scarcely any blood had been spilled from the wound.

Mrs Redman who had done the swabbing and bandaging herself, finally became conversational. 'I'm obliged to you for what you've done for us today. Also for seein' we got the money, intact. Things will be different in the future. Are you any good with cows?'

'I've worked on cattle ranches before, Mrs Redman. I could come back an' help in a day or so. Right now, you won't have a lot of work around the ranch, seein' as how you've jest disposed of a herd. I'll take these new hands back with me for this one trip, till we've sorted out the old hands. I'll bring the new boys back again before the end of the week.'

The old woman nodded soberly. 'It ain't a case of helpin' out. This outfit needs a strong man to ramrod it. One who can clean up the name of Redman for the future. I reckon nobody could make out a better case for the job than you, yourself. You'll think it over, will you?'

Rusty nodded. Mary murmured something about his having questions to ask. He was told that Old Man Redman had been dead for a few years: that the two sons of the marriage had been sent away over the border south by their mother around the time when renegade elements began to muscle in on Redman territory and the family reputation. The sons had never returned, and their mother had never blamed them for it.

Mary and the younger Alicia took up the conversation, giving further details of their family life, but Rusty was found to be sleeping with his chin propped on his hand. Alicia touched him lightly on the left shoulder, which caused his elbow to slide off the table and bring him back to wakefulness.

'You can sleep properly in a bed, if you want to,' the old woman offered.

'Maybe another time, ma'am. There's things waiting to be done in town right now.'

Five minutes later, he was in the saddle leading a new batch of prisoners and their escort into Redman City.

# 16

There was a great sorting out in the town of Redman City during the ensuing forty-eight hours. Harvey Prole's make-shift administration began to tick over. A celebrated townsman with legal qualifications was nominated as a temporary judge. Another twelve men acted as a jury. Ringo Redman and the other prisoners faced a short trial, with swift verdicts which were quickly ratified.

On the second morning after Rusty's visit to the Circle R, Ringo and six others were duly hung, one at a time, by Garrotty. It was not often in the west that a hangman ended up by hanging the official who sent for him to hang others.

Ten other men were jailed for a month, with a hard labour sentence to follow in Big Bend. Another eight were sharply cautioned and given a head start for the nearest border. They were warned never to return.

That same morning, Rusty sent the new cowpunchers back to the ranch with a message to say that he would be along himself that day or the next. Something was unsettling him. He did not fully understand himself, or what it was that he required to make him settle.

Maybe he could not stick the Circle R long enough to be of service to Laura's mother and sisters. Laura, he thought, there was the source of his trouble. He did not know where she was or when he would get to see her.

Around two in the afternoon, he took himself off on horseback, alone, determined to try and straighten out his thoughts on the present and the future. His need for solitude took him to the nearest spot on the local stream, Redman Creek.

★ ★ ★

At three o'clock precisely, a party of horse riders headed by a famous federal marshal entered Redman City, having come directly from Big Bend. Jason Windler, the marshal in question, was a tough bespectacled ex-Ranger in his middle fifties, who had never been known to back down on a difficult situation.

He had with him the less resolute county sheriff and a posse of ten men, finally prompted into making a show of force into Redman City. The call at Big Bend on the way had been an eye opener for the peace officers, who were still very impressed when they arrived in the liberated stronghold of the old Redman gang.

Jay Paris was in charge of the farm wagon purchased in Freedom Falls earlier. He had used it to bring along a family who wanted to move back into Redman City. He had orders of all sorts which would no doubt fill the vehicle to its full capacity for the return run.

Laura Burke and her brother-in-law

had reached Freedom Falls the day before Marshal Windler prompted this ride in force to Redman. After Rusty's departure, the young woman had not been able to settle. Her longing for him, and her conscience, which suggested that she ought to be back with her family sharing their trials and tribulations, caused her to ask Jabez to take her back west.

Burke and his sister-in-law were as amazed as any other visitors when they heard about and saw the changes wrought in the ghost town in so short a time. Everything was coupled with the name of Rusty Redman. The more she heard about him, the surer she was that she loved him.

Her excitement was intense on the way into Redman City. There was plenty for all the new arrivals to see, but within ten minutes Laura Redman Burke was deflated. The man she sought was not there. After a short but frantic search, followed by enquiries, Sailor Please admitted that he knew the direction of Rusty's ride.

She located the dappled grey, frisking about and flipping the flies off its back, in a belt of trees up from the creek. Leaving her black mare to get better acquainted with the grey, she moved off down the slope and seated herself at the foot of a tree, near the discarded clothing.

Rusty came out shortly afterwards, looking serene and fresh. He had dried himself and partially donned his clothes when a voice from behind a tree startled him.

'Well, howdy, Rusty? Folks do tell me you've got prospects in the world. Bright ones, too. Like bein' town marshal of Redman City, or an important person in Big Bend.'

Rusty's heart thumped. He grinned broadly. Now he knew why he had recently been so restless. Laura's absence had a lot to do with it. He willed himself not to rush round and embrace her.

'An oldish lady offered me the job as

foreman of the local ranch, the Circle R. That sounded interestin'.'

Laura chuckled. 'An ambitious young foreman might win himself a part of the holdings, if he married into the family.'

His hair was still tousled as he grabbed her into his arms. He whispered into her ear that such a course of action was quite a possibility.

## THE END

We do hope that you have enjoyed reading this large print book.

Did you know that all of our titles are available for purchase?

We publish a wide range of high quality large print books including:
**Romances, Mysteries, Classics**
**General Fiction**
**Non Fiction and Westerns**

Special interest titles available in large print are:
**The Little Oxford Dictionary**
**Music Book, Song Book**
**Hymn Book, Service Book**

Also available from us courtesy of Oxford University Press:
**Young Readers' Dictionary**
**(large print edition)**
**Young Readers' Thesaurus**
**(large print edition)**

For further information or a free brochure, please contact us at:
**Ulverscroft Large Print Books Ltd.,**
**The Green, Bradgate Road, Anstey,**
**Leicester, LE7 7FU, England.**
**Tel:** (00 44) **0116 236 4325**
**Fax:** (00 44) **0116 234 0205**

## KILLINGS AT LETANA CREEK

### Bill Williams

Retired United States marshal Ned Thomas rides to Letana Creek to help a friend who fears being the next victim of a serial killer. But Ned makes matters worse for his friend's family and puts his own life in danger. Ned will need all his guile to solve the mystery surrounding the killings and to confront the Molloy brothers, unexpectedly released from prison. They are hell-bent on revenge. But those who write him off as a has-been are sorely mistaken . . .